WHITEOUT

WHITE OUT

A SUSPENSE NOVEL

BRETT CAIN

Covenant Communications, Inc.

Cover image: *Young Man Standing in the Mist* © jxfzsy, courtesy of istock.com.

Cover design copyright © 2019 by Covenant Communications, Inc.

Published by Covenant Communications, Inc.
American Fork, Utah

Printed in the United States of America
First Printing: January 2019

26 25 24 23 22 21 20 19   10 9 8 7 6 5 4 3 2 1

ISBN 978-1-52440-584-7

To my family, with all my love

ACKNOWLEDGMENTS

THE GREATEST COMPLIMENT ANYONE CAN ever give is *thank you*. My editor is Kami Hancock. Her patience, encouragement, and correction proved invaluable. Toree Douglas designed this fine cover with great skill and attention. Sam Millburn and Kathy Jenkins have been unfailingly supportive of this new writer. My beloved friends were inspirational every step of the way. I thank them and many others, for everything.

CHAPTER ONE

THE THING ABOUT CAR CRASHES is that they are often avoidable and always devastating.

Mine was no exception.

People mistakenly call them accidents. *Accident* implies an unpredictable, unintended occurrence. An accident is pocket-dialing your mom or knocking over a glass of milk. I am not a stickler for legal terminology, but I like to think precise language counts for something. They are collisions, or crashes, if you like—usually unintended but always the result of someone doing something wrong.

Not that I much cared in the moment how the disaster was defined. Sometimes you see it coming and the precious billionths and trillionths of a second tick by in what seems slow motion. Except it's not always slow enough for your brain to assess, evaluate, and signal a saving reaction.

But I didn't see this one coming.

Not by a long shot.

I was driving through the west end of Montana in the middle of winter. The weather was even colder than I had expected. But I had a working heater and a smooth ride, a 1968 Buick Skylark, to be precise—a real classic, immaculately maintained by the previous owner until the day he died, whereupon he had, for some far too generous reason, bequeathed it to me.

I was a newly minted returned missionary. My reception had not been momentous. It wasn't that I'd wanted a lot of fanfare, but not even my family could be there. My brother was working overseas somewhere, my sisters were married and couldn't get away, and my folks were serving as missionaries themselves.

I like to keep a low profile anyway, so I was not overly dismayed.

After being released as a full-time missionary for The Church of Jesus Christ of Latter-day Saints and giving my report, my stake president had expressed interest in my dating his daughter. I was flattered. She wasn't. Again, I was not overly dismayed.

Then I went to see Jim Anderson, a homebound member of the ward—I had been his home teacher, back when there were such things as home teachers—but he had died. It was due to natural causes, incident to old age.

He had no relatives—just an attentive ward family. He had kept the Skylark in his garage, and under the windshield wipers had been a note scrawled on half a sheet of printer paper. It said, *For Sawyer*. He'd always called me by my last name. Everyone did.

Brother Anderson had often joked before I left that I would have a companion named Finn, as in Huckleberry.

I would prune his orchard and mow his lawn and stack his wood. I would ask about his past, and he would talk about my future. I liked his advice a lot. One thing he told me was not to worry about life . . . "Just live it," he said.

I had missed his funeral service by a day. So, with nothing else to do and as a sort of tribute to his memory, I'd decided to take a trip, a long drive to see the country I had missed for so long.

The Buick drove like a dream. Honestly, I felt a little ostentatious driving it. It was scarlet red with a buckskin interior. Against the backdrop of the winter set, it must have stood out like Rudolph's nose.

And it was fast. Whoever put it together must have subscribed to the theory that too much horsepower is barely enough. But I wasn't pushing her to top speeds. Not even close. Barely half the posted limit.

The snow fell in fat, silver-dollar-sized flakes. I was alone on the road and in no particular hurry, so the cautious crawl was no kind of bother. I had driven all the way from Seattle, stopping only to fill up with gas, which was more often than needed because of my almost inflexible habit of keeping the top half full. My dad always said it was just as easy to keep the top half full as the bottom half. It was a small price for peace of mind. The I-90 had been uneventful all the way from Seattle to Montana. Whereas the interstate traffic had been sparse, the mountain roads were downright deserted.

The songs on the radio turned to static. Not that there was much to listen to besides the AM station repeating weather conditions, which I found redundant because all anyone had to do to was look outside. There was plenty of snow piling and drifting across the road. The centerline was obscured by the swirling flurries, and flakes filled the windshield before being swept aside by the wipers one moment only to rally again the next.

The two-lane highway was bordered by token guardrails and ditches full of snow, beyond which lay stretches of open land leading to tree-lined hills.

The Buick followed my eyes, drifting to the side. I instinctively indicated my move by bumping the turn signal stalk, as if it were a lane change and not carelessness.

I meant to do that.

I was not worried about advising other motorists of my move; there were none. I needed something to help keep my drowsiness at bay. I rolled my window down for a freezing and effective awakening. Very refreshing. For a second. Then it got too cold, and I rolled it up in a hurry. After two years in South America, I was experiencing some serious climate shock.

Like the hero in Homer's *Odyssey*, I felt the Sirens' call to sleep, but there was nowhere to stop. Actually I counted myself to be stuck in the *Iliad* since I was headed toward Troy.

Troy, Montana, that is. A small but important distinction. Like Paris, Texas, or the Mt. Olympus in Washington State, not Greece.

Troy. A historic but perhaps grandiose name. There were less than a thousand citizens. I like small towns though. There is always some interesting tidbit of history, a hole-in-the-wall eatery or world-record-holding something-or-other.

It would be worth a visit.

Maybe.

But I never got there.

Because in that instant a silver sedan, invisible in the blizzard, sped by in the opposite direction. I had been drifting, both off to sleep and to the left again. Just a bit, but enough for us to clip each other.

My fault entirely.

We brushed sides, like strangers bumping shoulders on a busy city sidewalk. I had been going much slower than the other driver, but there was still plenty of impact. I rocked sideways, rattling like an ice cube in an empty glass.

I felt my door dent against my thigh, and I caught a fleeting glimpse of the other driver, wide-eyed and open-mouthed. I over-corrected, fishtailing across the snow. The Buick's right flank grazed the guardrail, and I bounced sideways and up, hitting my head on the roof. Spinning the wheel, I ended up in the wrong lane. I put on the brakes as gently as I could and gradually, gratefully stopped sliding. I bumped the shifter into park and just sat there shaking.

The windshield wipers kept wiping. I breathed raggedly.

It was a rush.

But not the good kind.

The big V8 idled, but my heart raced. I pulled my fingers off the wheel, like breaking icicles off a roof. I clenched and unclenched my fists to stop the shakes.

There was enough damage to warrant a call to law enforce-ment, exchange insurance information, and express concern without admitting fault. But I figured both vehicles were still drivable. Just some superficial damage.

I checked my rearview mirror for the other guy. He wasn't on the road.

Adrenaline, already as rich as oxygen in my blood, doubled as I leapt out into the frigid air. I ran thirty yards to where I could see a faint glow of taillights burning red against the snow. The driver had smashed through the guardrail and gone off the steep embankment.

His car sat at a crazy angle, edged on both left tires with the right side all the way up in the air. Miraculously it had missed every single tree. I jumped down into the deep drift.

The driver was crawling through the broken-out windshield.

"Hey, pal, hold on," I called.

The man was middle-aged, short, and compact. He looked capable enough but more than slightly concussed. His nose was bleeding, maybe from the impact of the airbag, and his forehead had the makings of a hefty bruise. Floundering in the snow, I managed to help him back to the idling Buick. Retrieving my warm winter coat from the back seat, I wrapped it around the guy. It was a little big on him, which was good. It was more like a blanket than a coat. Turning up the heat full blast, I patted his arm reassuringly.

"Don't move, buddy. You'll be all right."

I held up my left hand to my ear, with the thumb and pinky splayed in the pantomime of a phone. "You got a phone, sir? I want to call for help."

The guy eased back and closed his eyes. He looked like he had fallen asleep, but he shook his head once.

Great.

I had heard you're supposed to keep people with concussions alert, so I dug my thumbs behind his collarbone—a little pain to wake him up. He grimaced and opened his eyes, first wide then narrowing, like the aperture of a lens, trying to focus.

"Stay with me, pal," I said. "You got a phone, sir? I want to call for help," I repeated, a little louder and a little slower.

No response.

Maybe he had some sort of emergency roadside assistance button. I closed the door on him and dashed back to his car.

I didn't know much about cars. Even though I was driving a gearhead's dream, I hadn't paid the usual price for it of scraped knuckles, grease-stained clothing, and years of intensive work.

Climbing down the bank again, I approached the sedan. It was a new Chevy Caprice—silver, sleek, full-sized, and perfect for cruising, except in the snow, obviously. Odd banging noises and clicks came from the car, like it was, in fact, a ticking bomb. The heat from the undercarriage and the exhaust were melting the snow nearest the crash site.

I circled around to the front, clambered down, reached through the space where the windshield had been, and felt for the ignition. I found the key and turned the car off. The noises continued, the banging and clicking. Diving farther in, I looked all around the dash, the console, and next to the rearview mirror. I didn't see any sort of helpful buttons.

As I moved to slide back out of the car, I saw something. The eye can process visual stimuli in as little as thirteen milliseconds. The brain takes a little longer to register the stimuli, more so when the images are new or unexpected. Hence the double take.

On the passenger seat under a dusting of broken glass and deflated airbags were two dark, angry stains. I had seen more than the average person sees of blood in my life. Sometimes my own. Sometimes not. So I know it when I see it. And I was seeing it.

The blood was black and pooled, like when kids mix all their paint on a page, mingling the colors into shades of nothingness.

I didn't think it was the driver's. It was fresh but not that fresh. I've had my share of bad nosebleeds, and even the worst nosebleed doesn't drain away your life like that. I checked and rechecked the interior, looking for any more signs of life or death.

Nothing.

I scrambled back out to widen my search. Squinting against the sun, I looked for more blood in the snow. That is one good thing about snow. Color shows up clearly against it.

Nothing. No drips or drops or splattering trajectory. No shambling footprints or any pattern an injured and disoriented person might leave behind.

I expanded the perimeter of my search again. You always start close and work your way out from the source, like ripples in a pond.

And I saw it. Deep in the snow, a stone's throw away, a shape. It was out of place, motionless but not a rock or a stump or hillock and not yet entirely covered in snow. Most people might have approached slowly, tentatively, dreading what they might find but still drawn nonetheless by the inexplicable morbid curiosity. Before regretting it for the rest of their lives.

But I wasn't most people.

I ran to it. Sending up flurries of snow with each step, I came crashing to my knees at the side of a body. It was a man, splayed out like he'd been frozen halfway through making a snow angel.

I know CPR, and I've given first aid plenty of times, but it would have been no use.

Unlike Brother Anderson, this man had not died of natural causes, not from causes incident to old age. But he was just as dead.

I rolled the corpse over. It wasn't easy. The guy wasn't particularly large, but there is a reason it's called dead weight.

The wounds that had bled on the seat were big and obvious in his stomach and chest. He had not died instantly. That was clear from the size of the stains; his heart had been pumping until very recently. So he had been wounded elsewhere, died in the car, and finally catapulted into the snow.

I recognized him. Not personally but by reputation. He was dressed conservatively in a dark wool suit, blue shirt, and dark tie. He had a gold badge on his belt and an empty molded brown-leather shoulder holster.

He was an FBI agent.

Now I *really* needed to call 911.

I had inadvertently contaminated a crime scene. I turned around, looking back to the road, where a man I could only assume was the killer sat in my car wearing my coat.

Turning back to the fallen agent, I bent down and further disrupted the integrity of the scene by searching his pockets for a phone.

Later I would remember seeing a dark shape in my peripheral vision. I hadn't heard approaching footsteps; they must have been muted by the snow.

But what I didn't hear and barely saw I most certainly felt. A solid blow to the back of my head sent me down to all fours, half-turning toward my unknown assailant before I was hit again on the left side of the face.

The whitewashed world I had known went as black as the night's shadow. At least I didn't feel the cold anymore. And besides, I was very tired.

CHAPTER TWO

I DIDN'T KNOW HOW LONG I had been unconscious. Not too long, I figured, since I hadn't frozen to death. My sight was blurry, like opening your eyes under water or squinting really hard. Snow was still falling, and I could see blinking lights. They flashed blue and white and red. Like those gaudy Christmas lights some people leave up half the year.

I started the slow, painful process of sitting up—it felt like surfacing from a SCUBA dive—and gingerly felt my head. There was a bump on the back and a cut above my left eye.

A cop was standing on the road next to an SUV with flashing lights. He was looking at me and talking into his radio.

Now I felt the cold. Looking down, I saw the impression I had left in the snow, filling up quickly with fresh powder. The wrecked car had cooled. It wasn't making noises anymore.

I half-crawled, half-climbed up the embankment. Road flares spiked into the asphalt glowed with a spectral light, marking the crash site.

The cop stepped back, dropping a mittened hand to his gun.

"Don't move," he yelled. I stopped, and we sized each other up.

He was like a fully dressed snowman, made up of three distinct round portions. His chunky legs ballooned in heavy pants and boots. His sizable stomach was barely contained in a shiny coat, and above it all, instead of a corncob pipe and carrot nose, a youthful face was crammed into a furry hat.

"Take it easy," I said.

"Is that your car?"

I looked back at the crunched car in the ditch. The trunk had popped open, evidently a delayed reaction to the crash—probably some sort of safety feature, like automatically unlocking the doors.

"No, *that's* my car." I turned back, pointing behind the cop.

To an empty spot of highway.

Not good.

The cop looked around. "Where?"

"It's gone; the other guy must have taken it," I said. "Can you get an ambulance here or something? We've got somebody dead down there."

His face clouded with confusion like I was speaking gibberish. Maybe my head wound had rendered me incapable of speaking anything but Spanish and I couldn't tell the difference. I had heard of returned missionaries involuntarily reverting to their mission language mid-conversation.

"What guy? Who's dead? You drunk?"

At least he had understood my words, even if he didn't know what I meant.

I looked back and saw what he was seeing. Snow. The body was invisible now. Maybe I had been out longer than I had thought. Or maybe there was just a lot more snow.

"Where's the body?" the officer asked.

"He's in the snow." I pointed down the embankment. The snow seemed to fall faster.

He stood there for a minute, saying nothing. I could see the wheels turning behind his eyes. He was probably trying to decide what to do—scramble in the snow or get back into his nice warm rig.

I thought about producing my passport as ID—maybe if I showed him I had nothing to hide he would believe my story. But I didn't want to make any sudden movements, didn't want to reach for my pockets—not with the abominable snowman all anxious and unpredictable.

Eventually he came to a conclusion. And it was the wrong one.

He did some complicated motion with his right-hand mitten, pulling a Velcro strap and turning it into a fingerless glove. He then managed to produce his pistol, spread his feet wide, and extended his arms straight out. It took him so long I could have closed the distance and knocked him out just like had been done to me. The muzzle of the gun twitched; he was shaking hard. I could hear the slide rattling against the barrel. It could have been nerves. Could have been the cold. But I did nothing. Just waited to see what he would do next.

"Don't move. Put your hands up," he said, perhaps not realizing that those were, in fact, conflicting orders.

"What?"

"Freeze."

"I'm about to; aren't you?"

The cop looked perplexed. My wit was lost on him. But it tends to be on most people, so I couldn't blame him.

I held my arms out low, showing I was unarmed. "I'm not the bad guy," I said.

The cop reached down with one hand to his belt, pulling out a pair of handcuffs.

"You're under arrest."

I almost didn't argue. The chance of getting inside a heated car under any circumstances seemed better than being turned into the world's largest popsicle.

But I am contrary by nature. And I was innocent.

"For what?"

"Put your hands behind your back."

I didn't want to do that. Tell me to do something and I'm inclined to do the opposite. Usually. Especially when it comes to authoritarians. I am not anti-authority, not really. I just don't like the misapplication of authority. The abuse of it. I had spent two years following stringent yet righteous rules. I could tell the difference.

"There's a dead guy down there."

No reaction.

I tried again. "Someone hit me over the head and stole my car."

Again, no reaction. I was getting nowhere with this guy.

He moved forward, jangling the cuffs out in front of him, like a beggar and his cup.

It was too cold to stand there protesting. At least I wasn't ordered to lie on the frozen asphalt. I turned around with my hands interlocked behind me.

The cop didn't read me my rights. Just clicked the cuffs on and marched me to the back seat of his SUV. The red and blue lights strobed, turning the flakes into miniature fireworks. The decal on the side read *Cluff Police Department*. On the hood there was an escutcheon with the words *Protect and Serve*, which the cop was doing halfway. He was protecting me from the frostbite, but I didn't foresee any good customer service coming from him anytime soon. Inside, the heater was running at least. I felt myself begin to thaw, painfully. My numbed face and fingers prickled and tingled back to life. My head hurt, but not too badly. It wasn't the worst headache I'd ever had.

The cop got in, turned down his belt radio, and took the mic from a cradle on the dash.

"French, here. I've got one in custody."

He looked at me in the rearview mirror, raising his eyebrows like he expected me to protest.

I said nothing.

He turned sideways in his seat to face me. He was one of those guys who didn't look bad being fat. Like that was his normal, intended shape.

"You drunk or something?" the cop asked again, not accusingly, just like he was hoping for a more harmonious outcome. If I was impaired, then there might have been no basis for my story, which would spell a lot less paperwork and worry for him.

I said nothing. I didn't want to incriminate myself. Things could be misheard or misconstrued.

He took off his mittens, faced forward again, and started driving.

Relegated to passenger, or rather prisoner, I could take my eyes off the road. Out of the windows I had a pretty good view of the area. Not that there was much to see. Just snow.

Of course, I hadn't seen snow for two years.

The cop kept looking in the rearview mirror like he wanted to talk or like he was daring me to pose more questions.

I didn't speak. I just sat back and waited. I was ready to explain what had happened, but not to the abominable snowman. I felt like an irate customer. *I want to speak to a manager.* I figured I would soon meet someone in charge.

I came to the easy conclusion that the other driver had been the one who'd hit me and stolen my car. I wanted the cops to start looking soon. Of course, my car was pretty distinguishable, so the killer wouldn't get far. I hoped.

We drove along the darkening highway and turned toward the town. I probably would have missed the turnoff, as inconspicuous as it was. The road took a steep downward grade, and when I glanced out the windshield, it looked as if we were off-roading. There was no clear indication of the road. The hills and trees rose on either side of us like we were on a slow-motion slalom. After a while the road leveled out, and I caught a glimpse of an icy river in the middle distance. The hills and trees gave way just enough so I could see the sepia-toned street lights burning against the snowy night.

I was hoping I would get to see most of the small town on our drive to the police station. Despite the less-than-ideal circumstances surrounding my visit, I was looking forward to being somewhere I'd never been. Except I had never been to jail before, and I wasn't over the moon about that.

I had a cousin who was a travel agent. Perhaps I should have spoken to her before planning this trip.

I caught a sideways glimpse of the welcome sign. Snow had drifted up against it and piled high on top of it, but I could see the number of residents was nine hundred and fifty-eight. *And,* it added in curly script, *three old grouches.*

Which I appreciated. Honesty is the best policy. Usually.

Most towns make the first few blocks the best—a warm welcome—with the nicest stores, the best restaurants, and the prettiest parks. Not exactly tourist traps but definitely calculated to attract. I expected a small historic center, a roadhouse-style restaurant, and maybe a mom-and-pop general store.

But I didn't get to see any of that. The police station came first. Maybe it was meant to serve as a sign of safety to visitors, a reassurance.

Or a warning, to frighten off undesirables.

I didn't know. It neither reassured nor dismayed me.

The station was big. Bigger than it needed to be, considering the population. For a town with nine hundred and sixty-one folks in it, I would imagine one middling sheriff with a couple of volunteer deputies could keep all the peace there was to be had.

But what did I know? The citizens had obviously signed off on the department budget. It was their tax dollars at work.

Then I saw it was not just for police use. It was like an entire civic center, with everything from a police department to a post office. It had everything people needed and plenty they didn't.

We drove under a giant archway made up entirely of bleached-white antlers.

I'd never been hunting. Didn't interest me. There was just something unappealing about the whole pageantry of the thing—wearing camouflage, making fake mating calls, shooting things.

Not for me.

You kill a lion with your bare hands? Good for you.

Blow the head off a snake before it strikes? Cool.

But shoot an unsuspecting herbivore with a high-powered rifle from a comfortable distance? I'm not impressed. Of course, I'm no conservationist. Not by any stretch of the imagination. I'm not an animal rights activist or a vegetarian. I like meat as much as the next guy. So I can understand and respect subsistence hunting.

I would just rather hunt something that could fight back, make it a fair fight.

I thought the officer would bring me to the rear of the building to the jail, where I would be booked and fingerprinted. *Processed,* they called it, like it was the same as being put into one of those big blenders used for making smoothies and salsa and chutney.

Maybe here they hadn't upgraded to the digital machines and they would cover my hands in ink. Maybe I would have to hold up one of those numbered signs and get my picture taken.

Instead the cop pulled to a stop in front of the building, leaving the engine running. He heaved his bulk out and trekked around to my door. Opening it, he stepped back. With some difficulty I scooted along the seat and hooked my feet on the bottom lip of the door frame to pull myself out of the vehicle. He marched me up the steps, both of us trying not to slip, both of us relying on the other for balance. He needed to keep me up because I had my hands behind my back, and I needed to keep him standing so he didn't fall on me.

He had been walking behind me, holding my elbow, but as we came to the door, he turned me around so I was facing back the way we had come. I took a good look just in case this was going to be all I got to see of Cluff. He opened the door with one hand and pulled me through with the other.

We stepped into a spacious lobby with posts and beams and exposed rafters and hard, dark rosewood everywhere; community advisory boards and notices and wanted posters were surrounded with more antlers and animal pelts. An actual fire burned in a circular pit in the center of the wide room. I felt as though I were in an expensive hotel with a rustic western theme. With any luck, the police station would be complete with a five-star restaurant. I was hungry.

The front desk was empty. It was well after business hours.

An inconspicuous door opened up behind the counter, and a very conspicuous man came through. He stepped out from around the desk, running a hand through sandy hair, an impressive moustache bristling. He looked like he came straight out of a John Wayne movie.

"Chief," French said, letting go of my arm and stepping back like he didn't want to be in the way of whatever was in store for me.

"Take those cuffs off him, French."

The chief spoke evenly—no barking orders. He was just a guy who said things, and then they happened.

Officer French paused, mumbled something—perhaps an apology to me or the chief—and dug in his pocket for the keys.

He freed me without another word. The chief beckoned French with one hand and motioned for me to stay put with the other. The two exchanged a quick whispered conversation. I didn't hear what was said. French then turned to walk back out into the snow, presumably to park his still-running vehicle. Or go back on patrol. It looked too dark and snowy out to send a tow truck back to recover the wreck.

The patch above the chief's pocket read, *W. Strawn*. He was a big man and light on his feet. Unassuming but imposing. He had command presence. I almost saluted. He stuck out a big, calloused hand.

I shook it once.

"Bill Strawn." His voice was rumbly and deep but not unfriendly. "I'm sorry about that. French is new, and you can't be too careful in our line of work."

"Frank Sawyer," I said. "It's no problem."

We stood there in a semi-awkward silence—the kind that could permeate any unusual interaction between two strangers. I was happy to just be in the warm, aesthetically pleasing ambience.

Strawn looked slightly perturbed, like he had a whole laundry lists of problems and wasn't quite sure where I fit on it.

"Can I offer you some coffee?" He asked.

"Got hot chocolate?"

"Sure. Follow me."

I followed Strawn back around the desk and through the door into the squad room. There was a pair of percolators on a counter behind the desks. A stainless-steel sink had some leftover dishes and mugs stacked in it, like a miniature cutout of a kitchen. Strawn pulled a Styrofoam cup from a stack and handed it to me. He reached into a drawer and pulled out a small tin of cocoa powder. It was not a brand name I recognized, but I was prepared to like it.

As I made my cup of cocoa, Strawn stood by, his big hands on his narrow hips.

"I'm afraid we do have some questions for you."

I blew steam from the piping brew. "I sure hope so."

Strawn motioned me forward. "Come with me to my office."

I was a little surprised but not at all displeased with his hospitality as opposed to the low-grade hostility I'd experienced from French. I had anticipated being jerked around before I could get my side of the story out. I'd imagined having to fill out witness statements, signing and dating here and there and having photocopies made of my government-issued identification. All I had was my passport. My driver's license had long since expired. But Strawn seemed to take it for granted that I was the victim, and protocol appeared to be flexible.

I followed him through the squad room, past the hardwood desks. The chairs were ergonomic masterpieces, replete with knobs and mesh and adjustable back supports. The office felt like a lounge in an exclusive club. The furniture looked like the kind that would be found in the finest of ivy-league libraries, not the utilitarian composite material junk you see in regular offices. Clearly the budget had line items for more than just personnel.

I had never wanted an office job, but if I had to have one, I could see myself enjoying a place like this.

No one else was in the building as far as I could tell. Everyone was likely either off duty or on patrol. Probably the former, I figured.

Freezing-cold weather was usually an excellent crime deterrent—nothing to see on a night like this. Besides my crash and a murder.

I waited for Strawn to sit down behind his desk before sitting myself.

Strawn steepled his fingers on the desk.

"Tell me the story, Mr. Sawyer."

So I explained about my drive and the snow and the cold. I described the deserted highway and my unhurried pace across his jurisdiction. I didn't mention my drowsiness. I didn't want to be arrested all over again for distracted driving, especially without a license. Honesty is the best policy. Usually. Withholding certain elements of information is not the same thing as lying. It's a matter of disclosure.

I told him about the sudden appearance of the speeding car. The accident. I mean *collision*. I told him how I had helped the dazed driver into my car and then had gone looking for a way to call for help. If he was surprised I didn't own a phone, he didn't show it. I told him about the bloodstains, the discovery of the agent's body, and the sneak attack on me

Strawn listened, not asking any questions, not taking notes, only nodding occasionally.

But I had a few questions of my own. "How did you find me?"

Strawn shrugged. "We received a call from a guy. He said he was a long-haul trucker and he thought he saw something out of place. He gave us the mile marker and nothing more."

"Why did you let me go?" I asked.

He shrugged. "You're clearly not drunk. You've committed no crime, not in my jurisdiction anyway."

"There's a body out there, a federal agent's to be precise," I said. "French refused to investigate it."

Strawn sighed. "You needn't spell out the gravity of the situation to me, son. I know how serious this is. I must say you're handling it well. Most people are catatonic after seeing something like that. Believe me, we are going to use all the technical ability and resources at our disposal. You'll have to excuse Officer French; he just got through field training. If you want to make a formal complaint, I'll give you the form."

"No. I'm not bitter. I don't really blame him, honestly. But there is a murderer on the loose with my car, and I don't see a lot of hurry to catch him."

He pointed to my head. "You want some ice on that?"

I shook my head, only slightly, because the motion brought echoes of dull pain. "It's plenty cold outside already. And it's not the worst I've ever had. I'll be fine."

Strawn nodded. "Well, I'd say you're lucky to be alive either way."

He was right. I was lucky. But not for having survived a little whack on the noggin. I had been in and out of plenty of scrapes and close calls, and this figured close to the least of them.

"What's the plan for catching him?" I asked.

He ignored my question. "What do you do for work, son?"

"At the moment, nothing. I was a missionary for the last couple of years, in Peru."

"And now you're not?" he asked.

"Correct," I said.

"You lose your faith?"

"No, sir, it's only a two-year commitment."

"Mormon?" he asked.

"Through and through."

"Where is it you're headed?" Strawn asked.

This is where I had not wanted the conversation to go. Because I didn't have a good answer.

I shrugged. "Nowhere in particular. Like I said, I just came back from Peru. I hadn't driven for two years, and I don't have any family close by, so I figured I would do a little exploring."

"Where are you from?"

"The Seattle area," I said.

The hint of a shadow passed over his eyes, like maybe he didn't like the Seahawks at all. Understandable. I can't stand them either. But as far as I knew, Montana didn't even have a National Football League team. Or maybe, like a lot of landlocked folks, he had a dim view of coasters. Which I could also understand. Or maybe it was nothing. Or maybe it was something else entirely.

"I'm not involved in any of this though," I said.

"Why would you feel the need to say something like that?" he asked.

"Because it's all just so coincidental, isn't it? I don't know about you, but I don't like coincidences. I mean, what are the odds you would have two out-of-towners—the FBI guy and me—show up at once? I mean, no offense, but this place isn't exactly Jackson Hole."

"I don't see any semblance of a coincidence. You weren't even headed for Cluff itself, and the car you crashed with was going the other way. Who's to say your attacker wasn't a visitor as well?"

He had a point. Maybe the bad guy hadn't even come from Cluff. Maybe he hadn't even driven back this way once he had stolen my car.

Strawn stood up slowly. Interview over.

"Mr. Sawyer, you're not a suspect. Relax. Enjoy your stay in our small town. We'll find the guy; he won't get far, whichever way he went."

I stood up, too, and gulped the last of the chocolate. I wasn't going to stay here and argue, running the risk of wearing out my welcome and having him change his mind.

"You got a hotel here? Maybe a good diner?"

"Motel, actually. Just a couple blocks from Main Street. Let me show you."

He showed me a map tacked to the wall behind my seat. The town was weird, zoned out in a circular fashion. The station was at the center, and from there twelve roads branched out like numbers on a clock or spokes on a wheel. The way French had brought me in was the twelve o'clock spoke. None of the streets were exactly straight—they meandered and wound a bit—but the four biggest were exactly oriented north, east, south, and west. Or the twelve, three, six, and nine o'clock positions.

Maybe the city planner had been Parisian or a clockmaker or a wheelwright. But whatever; it was not as good as Utah's grid system, but it made some kind of sense. Apart from the spokes were three inner rings, widening out like ripples in a well. Strawn showed me where we were and that the motel was about the equivalent of six blocks along the eleven o'clock spoke, right about halfway up the road's length.

He continued. "And as far as food goes, you can't do better than the Oak Table Café. Besides, it's the only show in town. Open late. It's west of here." He pointed a few blocks down, the nine o'clock spoke. "I can call French back to drive you."

"I'll walk, work up an appetite." I was already plenty hungry; I just didn't want to see French again so soon.

"Suit yourself. You know the way out?"

"Yes, sir. Thanks again."

I didn't really know why I was thanking him. Maybe for the cocoa. Or for not arresting me. At any rate, it seemed like a nice thing to say. Nice but inaccurate. Like a lot of the things people say. I had not thanked him at all before.

Nice but inaccurate. That could have easily been my high-school yearbook caption.

I went back out into the main lobby. It didn't strike me like a resort anymore. More like a lodge on a lake. First impressions can be lasting, but they are often wrong. The fire, burning low, emanated a soft, inviting kind of heat. Homey, like a warm hearth where a big dog might lie next to a pair of work boots. I would have liked to linger a bit, but I had been excused, and sustenance is more important than aesthetics every time.

I saw the other side of the front desk, where a sergeant probably sat during regular hours, with papers and other office supplies. There was a glossy photograph of a guy with a buddy, both dressed in white snow camouflage. From a hunting trip, evidently. One of them had shot a deer. They were smiling. The deer wasn't. An acetate name plate on the desk read, *SGT. LANG.*

I wondered where he fell on the scale of competency— somewhere between greenhorn French and veteran Strawn? A good cop, I expected. Most of them are.

CHAPTER THREE

WALKING OUT INTO THE FROZEN night, I was bludgeoned yet again. But not by an unseen assailant. Or rather, exactly by an unseen assailant. This time it was by bitter, brutal cold, and it was worse than the last one because I stayed conscious. I half-considered going back and asking for a ride. But my pride and stoicism forbade it.

I figured out exactly which way I was facing and struck out for the Oak Table Café. I walked toward the glow, taking to the center of streets because the sidewalks would have put me knee-deep in snow.

And it just kept on falling.

I passed below the conical beams of the street lights, trying to think warm thoughts. My breath fogged in front of me, and my lungs burned with frozen air.

From a side street, headlight beams flashed, and for a fraction of a second, I thought it was my own car, returning to me like KITT from *Knight Rider*, indestructible.

But it was a cop car. An officer I didn't recognize drove by, and following in the direction of the station, in his SUV, was French.

I instinctively raised my arm in greeting. He waved back.

Not a bad guy after all.

I wasn't trying to get the guy to fall in love with me, but no salutation is ever wasted. My mission had been all about being friendly and kind to everyone, no matter what. Even though I wasn't brimming with gratitude over the arrest, the fact was French had saved me from a very dangerous situation.

I found the eatery without incident, besides being cold.

The parking lot was empty, except for a burned-orange Jeep covered in snow.

The door was thick and heavy, with a big handle and a small fogged-up window. I stepped through, stamping my boots on the worn mat. A bell chimed.

Café was a bit of misnomer, in my opinion. *Café* implied small metal chairs and round tables in a courtyard partitioned off by a two-foot-high fence, with a menu of morsels. Or maybe that was a bistro or osteria. It seemed somewhere between a roadhouse and fine dining. Maybe. I didn't really know. I was no expert.

But whatever. This place seemed to be a full-fledged restaurant, which worked just fine for me.

But it was empty.

There was a sign on a brass pole that asked me to please wait to be seated. And I did. From the entryway, I could see just a little way into the main seating room as well as part of the kitchen and some booths and tables.

A young woman, about my age, poked her head inquisitively around the corner leading to the kitchen. She blew an errant strand of red hair out of her face, giving me a tired smile.

"Sit anywhere you'd like. I'll be right there."

Which is exactly how the wait-to-be-seated sign should have read. It made for a much better invitation.

"Thank you, miss."

I picked a corner booth against the kitchen wall and sat sideways so I could watch the door and the windows that took up two walls. It was too dark to see anything outside, but it made me feel better.

The interior was a lot like the station but less ornate, which was a better fit, given the log-cabin style. It was less pretentious, more functional. It had more blonde wood than dark. It was also devoid of any animal parts, which was another point in its favor.

The tables and chairs were wooden, the seats padded with cracked vinyl. The ceilings looked like freshly fallen trees stripped of their bark and branches and covered in a quick coat of sheen.

On the opposite wall a late model television was silently rebroadcasting the local news.

Leaning my head back against the wall and closing my eyes, I exhaled slowly. My headache had receded into a halfhearted throb, and the warmth of the restaurant was making me sleepy.

My car was gone. A setback, certainly, but it was by no means catastrophic. I had cash in my pocket and clothes on my back. Plenty of better people than me have gotten by with much less. I had met a lot of them in Peru.

I was grateful I was going to be free to see the rest of Cluff, and I was more grateful to be spared another day. I thought of the agent. What had he wanted to do? Where had he wanted to visit? Did he have a family?

I said a silent prayer and opened my eyes.

The girl was standing there, looking at me with a wry grin.

I sat up too quickly, and it made my head hurt.

"If you're looking for the motel, it's about six blocks that way." She pointed toward the windows on the back wall.

I smiled. "I'll get there eventually, I'm sure. But not on an empty stomach."

She smiled back, tilting her head to one side slightly. She looked like she came straight out of a storybook—short, slightly round, apple-cheeked, and fair-skinned, with a heavy dusting of freckles. Like cinnamon on porridge. Under dark eyes her nose sloped down into a button shape. Her mouth was a little wide, which suited her smile.

She set a single sheet of laminated paper in front of me that must have been the menu. I slid it right back to the edge of the table like a poor poker player folding before even glancing at his hand.

I was hungry, but since she was apparently working by herself, I didn't want to put her out. And I probably could have eaten one of everything listed.

Maybe two.

"How are your pancakes?" I asked.

"The best."

I believed her. Just like I believe every waitress. Because the best pancakes are always the ones you're eating at the moment.

"I'll take a short stack, please."

"Coffee?"

"Hot cocoa, please, if you have it."

She nodded and smiled, which seemed to be a habit of hers, and disappeared back into the kitchen. I settled back into my seat, trying to remember if she had had a nametag. I could have drifted off then and there, but I have always endeavored to never go to bed on an empty stomach. And mostly I've succeeded.

Keep the top half full.

I tried to imagine where the investigation was headed on the murder victim and my stolen car. More likely than not Chief Strawn would be trying to identify the body, burning up the phone lines calling the FBI. Homicide tended to take precedence over grand theft auto in our crazy, mixed-up world of skewed priorities.

A few minutes later the girl came back with a plate of thick, fluffy pancakes as big as hubcaps. They were golden-brown with a perfect square of butter melting before my eyes. She slid the plate in front of me and with her other hand set a thick ceramic mug of steaming cocoa on the table. She handed me a set of cutlery from her apron, rolled in a paper napkin.

No name tag, which was a pity. I like to learn people's names.

"Thank you very much."

"May I join you?"

"Of course." I was a little taken aback, but in a good way. As she sat down, I disregarded the knife and cut into the stack with the edge of my fork.

She set her elbows on the table and crossed her arms.

"What happened to your face?"

I looked at her in mock horror, eyes wide. "What's wrong with it?"

She laughed.

"I got hit. It happens from time to time."

"Sorry about that."

"It wasn't your fault."

"You're either really lucky or really not."

Between careful mouthfuls of pancake, I smiled. I am not a self-conscious eater, but when in the company of a lady, it is best to avoid talking with your mouth full. Or letting butter run down your chin.

"After tasting these, I would say really lucky."

She laughed. "'Be no flatterer.'"

"I'm sorry?" I said.

"George Washington's *Rules of Civility and Decent Behaviour.*"

"You've read them?" I asked, surprised. Not many people were familiar with the first American president's pocket-sized book of guidelines.

"Don't look so shocked. I can read, you know." She was joking, but maybe she had met out-of-towners who thought all backwoods beauties working in diners were illiterate.

"'Be no flatterer.' That one's the seventeenth rule. It goes on to say not to tease those who don't want to be," I said, with a bit of satisfaction. It pays to be well-read.

"*You've* read them?" she said, and I wasn't sure she was joking. Maybe she thought young male victims of car thievery with bad haircuts and no coats couldn't read.

"I can read too. A little."

"I'm glad you don't mind being teased." She smiled again.

"I don't mind anything when I'm eating food this good," I said, taking another bite.

"Well, good food or not, I would say you're lucky and unlucky. Lucky to have gotten into town at all and not so much being stuck here." She unfolded her arms and spread her hands on the tabletop. I didn't see a ring, which should have been the thing I looked for before a name tag.

"What do you mean?" I asked around another mouthful.

"An hour before sundown the eastbound mountain pass closed. Completely snowed in. An hour after that the road west was shut down. Looks like you'll be here for the duration of the storm."

Strawn hadn't mentioned that. Maybe that was why he wasn't in a rush. He knew the murderer-thief couldn't go anywhere.

A matter of disclosure.

I shrugged and smiled. "I wouldn't get very far at the moment anyway."

"Why's that?"

"My car was stolen."

"You're kidding."

"I wish I was." I indicated the bruise and cut.

I didn't mention the body. Didn't seem an appropriate dinner topic.

I switched targets and drank a bit of the hot chocolate. It was good. Better than the police station's. Setting the mug back on the table, I turned back to the pancakes. I would have liked to have just talked with the waitress, but I was hungry and figured I could at least listen to her. Which was probably a whole lot better than rambling on myself.

"I'm sorry."

I gestured dismissively with the fork. "Not your fault. If that is the worst thing that ever happens to me, then I'm the luckiest guy in the world."

I took another bite. "Besides, like I said, it's hard to get all bent out of shape about anything with pancakes like these."

The waitress smiled and shook her head. "You're pretty cavalier with your praise."

"Just calling them like I see them. How do you get them so fluffy anyway?"

"Oh, it's an ancient recipe passed down from generation to generation. Only those worthy of such knowledge are initiated," she said, pausing for effect. "I'm just kidding; it's actually really easy. You just put a lid over them while they cook, and the heat kind of steams them."

"Good to know."

Her eyes had just a touch of shyness. But the shrewd kind of shy, like she knew her strengths and her weaknesses. She was self-assured, self-possessed. A heck of a girl. With an easy smile. Probably the best I had seen in a long time. I hadn't seen anyone like her in more than two years.

We just sat there for a moment, both smiling, both saying nothing.

"I'm Mary, by the way."

Inwardly I cheered. It was always better to let girls give you their name without having to ask for it. Otherwise you might come across as being too forward.

I set my fork down and stuck out my hand. "Frank Sawyer. Pleased to meet you."

She smiled again. "Frank? That's kind of an old man's name, right? I mean, no offense."

"None taken. It's true. Both of my granddads were Frank. Short for Franklin on my mom's side and Francis on my dad's."

"So, which are you?"

"Neither. Just Frank, but most people call me Sawyer."

"Okay. Sawyer, then. I like that better. 'Frank' just sounds too old."

"Just how young do you think I am?"

"Younger than me, and I'm twenty-two."

I grinned, but I didn't correct her. Flattering, but she was mistaken. *Nice, but inaccurate.*

"So, what are you going to do about your car?"

Finishing off my pancakes, I eased back in my seat. It was a good question. One I did not have an answer for. Which was all right because, in that moment, the heavy door sighed open, and a rush of frigid air spilled in. The bell above the lintel—loud, intrusive, and rude—interrupted our cozy, intimate moment between two perfect strangers.

In my relatively short earthly sojourn, I had managed to subdue a number of the evolutionary habits so pervasive to our kind. Take, for instance, when something makes a sound out of sight—it is the reflex of every creature that sees better than hears to look toward the source.

Mary looked.

I didn't.

Not that there is an innate advantage to *not* looking. Quite the opposite, really. This was just another instance of my immense pride manifesting itself in odd ways. I didn't like the idea of gratifying whoever came through that door with two pairs of surprised eyes. The peripheral worked just as well. And besides, I really couldn't take my eyes off Mary. I liked her. A lot.

So I didn't look. I just leaned back and drained my cup of cocoa. I made out two distinct shapes trudge inside amid a heavy shower of snow. One was French, the guy who had arrested me. The other was something else, a good two inches above my six feet and a solid twenty pounds on top of my two hundred and ten. Across the cheekbones, he looked Indian—that is to say, Native American, not from the subcontinent in Asia. He was dark and handsome, with a shock of thick black hair. Reminded me of Elvis.

Mary smiled and stood up, taking my plate. "Hi, Carter. Hi, Rock. The usual?"

They nodded. Kept staring at me. Small towns are always clannish and sometimes hostile. I had seen that on my mission—I had often been the only non-native in towns and villages in the jungle and mountains, and I had often felt the disapproving non-attention. But that can be part of the challenge, if not the charm. I like winning hearts and minds, and I like the relative peace and quiet of country living as opposed to the neon wash, the exhaust-filled air, and the press of people under glittering structures that blot out the sky.

The men moved toward the center of the room, decreasing the distance, trying to catch my eye.

I still hadn't bothered to look directly at them; I was too busy squaring my mug up in front of me, admiring the craftsmanship and width of the rim and hoping for a bottomless cup policy.

They might have taken me for diffident, too afraid to look them in the eye.

But I think they knew better. It was at once innocent obliviousness and a direct affront to their assumed alpha roles in the community.

Mary brushed my arm with her fingertips as if to say, *Be right back.* Or possibly, *Please don't break anything, because it will come out of my paycheck and I'll have to clean it up anyway and I was just starting to kind of, sort of, like you.* Or maybe nothing at all.

Finally I paid the men a lazy glance.

French was out of uniform, stuffed into a police academy sweat suit with his name embroidered on the front. He still looked a bit like a snowman, but he looked more at ease than he had been when he had arrested me. Rock was in identical apparel. The name embroidered on his outfit was actually *Roca*, which is Spanish for rock. Rock had a sort of veiled malevolence I didn't understand. We hadn't even met. I thought about asking if I might join them for their next gym session. I hadn't lifted weights in two years. But Rock looked like he might have abandoned me on the bench press with four hundred pounds on the bar.

I didn't move. Didn't blink. Just faded into a long, bleary stare, which wasn't hard to fake because, though my headache was packing up and moving out without much fanfare, the pancakes had been hearty, and I was dead tired. Plus, Mary's voice had such a relaxing, husky warmth to it that I was as ready to nod off as I'd ever been.

They were starting to look foolish, standing there in their sweatpants. Rock and French looked at each other, then back at me, and then toward the kitchen to make sure Mary was still gone. Finally Rock opened the ball.

"Hey."

I didn't answer.

At that moment, with me sitting and them standing, they had a distinct tactical advantage. But they weren't armed. Weapons are impossible to conceal in pocket-less, form-fitting sweat suits. They had nothing up their sleeves, but I did—the only thing I've ever needed in my arsenal: me.

While subduing evolutionary habits, I had cultivated another. In the moment Mary had looked to the front door, I had slid, almost imperceptibly, to the end of the bench and hooked my heel on the outside of the seat. I'd straightened up against the backrest and gotten ready for immediate action. There was nothing worse than being stuck in your seat. Not that I wanted or expected to fight, not at the moment, but the one thing I had taken away from years in Boy Scouts was the importance of being prepared. And the one thing I had taken away from my attack on the highway is that you can never get complacent.

People are always erratic and unpredictable.

Then the cops gave up the high ground. The actual high ground, that is, not the moral one. Not that I had much claim to that one either; in this case, I was just being a little petty.

Rock slid in across from me with the dexterous ease of a big, strong man, and French fumbled his bulk around, scooting and sliding until he was situated.

They each set their crossed arms on the table, sending tiny vibrations through my mug.

Rock spoke first. "I said, 'Hey,' whitey."

"I heard you. I don't know what you want though." I spoke evenly, slowly, and clearly, like a tired but patient parent listening to a kid whine.

Rock leaned harder on his arms. The table would have flipped if it hadn't been fixed to the floor. "What are you doing here?" he asked.

I gestured dramatically around me like a magician revealing the results of his magic. "Eating," I said. "Or I would end up all scrawny like you."

"Hilarious." He snorted and bunched his muscles. Maybe to prove to himself as well as to me that he was no tadpole.

"Just calling them like I see them," I said.

"Well, you're not welcome here." He looked at me hard.

"Where?" I asked.

"Anywhere."

"Well, your candor is most refreshing. As soon as you find my car, I will be on my way."

If it came to it, I could have fought them. I imagined myself knocking their heads either together or one at a time against the tabletop. French would be slow, and Rock would have been trapped in the booth between the wall and his partner's immovable girth until he could wriggle out from under the table, by which time I could have either escaped or put him out of action too.

But that was unnecessary. The imagined scenario was just the product of a brain programmed to assess every man like a potential enemy and figure out how, if needed, to beat them. It was an exercise that had become an instinct. Not that I looked for fights. Not at all. But if it ever came down to it, I couldn't waste time deciding whether or not I was going to fight. That was a choice I'd have to make long beforehand. Otherwise I'd already be too late.

I said nothing. I'm not much for trash talk. I prefer to fight with my hands.

"What's your problem?" I asked.

"We don't like strangers," French chimed in, but it didn't sound convincing from him.

"Me neither," I said. That gave them pause. I almost could hear the wheels in their heads grind. They were unable to form a verbal comeback.

"You afraid of us?" Rock asked.

I am afraid of nothing. But my pride does not stretch as far as rising to every challenge issued by each hothead I meet.

Suddenly I reached for my pocket. They stiffened and reeled back, thinking maybe I was going for a weapon.

I wasn't.

I set my passport on the table. They stared at it.

I opened it to the most recent stamp.

"I'm not afraid of you," I said. "I'm not amused either. I'm not annoyed with, interested in, or dismayed by you. I'm not your enemy. Those were the first pancakes I've eaten in two years. Mary is the first girl I've spoken to socially in two years. Now, if you want to eat, be my guest. I'm happy to buy you dinner. I like law enforcement. A lot. You saved me out there, French. Thank you."

French looked sheepish. "I'm sorry I arrested you right away."

"No apology needed," I said. "But there's a dead guy at the crash site and a murderer running around in my car."

Rock frowned. "You should have told French right away the DOA was a fed."

"It shouldn't have mattered what he was; it certainly didn't to the dead guy. A life is a life," I said.

They said nothing.

I put my passport back into my pocket and continued. "Now, what's the plan for catching the murderer?"

"No way he could have gotten anywhere going west. We put out an all-points bulletin right away, and the snow would have stopped him. We expect he came back this way, so he's snowed in. There's no point in us running around in the dark turning over every stone. He'll show himself sooner or later. You just stay out of our way, and maybe we'll get your car back for you," Rock said. He glowered at me until Mary came back with their meals. Then he was suddenly all smiles.

Now I understood the malevolence. I was a new competitor.

French's was an omelet devoid of any vegetables and replete with about two pounds of cheese. Rock's was a meatball sub.

Mary was frowning a fraction at the three of us, not liking the veiled enmity, evidently. Maybe she had some sort of extrasensory perception or womanly intuition, or maybe it just showed in our faces. I took that as my chance for a graceful withdrawal and tactical retreat from the verbal fray. As I slid out of the booth, I handed her a twenty-dollar bill.

"Keep the change," I said.

"Thank you."

"I'll be back for breakfast."

"We open at eight."

"Until then, Mary."

Without a backward glance at the sweat-suited pair of cops, I stepped out into the world's biggest freezer.

CHAPTER FOUR

I WAS COMFORTABLY CERTAIN THEY wouldn't follow me to pursue the debate. Not with Mary's cooking and company in front of them. I might have pushed too hard when disparaging their policing prowess. Chief Strawn seemed like a smart guy, but so far I wasn't making any friends out of his underlings. French was fine, but I figured he would defer to Rock's poor example. I'd have to try harder. It was not a good idea to wear out my welcome too soon. Especially since, according to Mary, I was stranded indefinitely.

The icy air pawed and clawed at me. I kept my hands in my armpits. Flakes were no longer falling, having called a temporary ceasefire. There was a tangible sense of silence after a heavy snow. Even freezing my face off, I could appreciate the quiet. Silence may or may not be golden, but it sure is peaceful. A lot of people have an ingrained aversion to silence. They seem to feel some sort of moral imperative to fill it. I like it though. If I had to, I think I could go the rest of my life without saying another word.

I plodded along, my boots heavy. They were solid items, by far the most expensive things I wore. They held up well in the snow. But whereas they were waterproof, my jeans were not. Halfway up my shins the snow had stuck, melted, and refroze in lumpy patches. By the time I reached the motel office door, my pant legs were stiff with cold.

The motel was a two-story utilitarian structure. No attempt had been made to match the decor I had seen at my previous stops. There was no shine, no polish. Just an office sandwiched between the rows of rooms—ten on either side, split between top and bottom. Only two vehicles sat in the lot. A semitruck with no load lay lengthwise across several parking slots and was neighbored by a van with chains on its wheels.

So, there's definitely a vacancy.

I wondered if this trucker had been the same to phone in my predicament, in which case I owed him. He had saved my life.

I stepped into the office, stomping my feet on the mat. It was only slightly warmer inside. No heater was running. I wondered how Spartan the accommodations themselves would be. Recessed lighting dimly illuminated the small space. A wooden shelf held brochures of the local attractions, which were few. A high counter held a ledger, and behind it hung a row of mail slots and a board with twenty hooks holding eighteen brass keys. A door behind the counter opened, and a big-boned black guy stepped out, pulling on an exceptionally well-worn sheepskin coat. He closed the door behind him. Maybe he kept the heat on only in his office to save money. He looked more cut out for cop work than either Rock or French. He had a shaved, glistening head and heavy-lidded eyes framed by wire-rimmed spectacles.

He raised a supermarket chicken-sized hand in greeting, straightening his glasses with the other.

"Hello," he said.

"Howdy," I said.

"Room?"

"Yes, please."

"Twenty dollars."

I produced a ten and two fives from my wad of cash. "Heck of a deal."

He tipped his head back to look at me out of the bottom of the lenses. "We don't see many folks in the wintertime. Summertime rate is sixty a night. We're always full then. Have to turn people away."

I nodded. I couldn't think of anything to say.

He opened the leather-bound ledger and spun it around to face me. Licking his finger, he flipped through the pages until he came to the newest. He handed me a fountain pen. I liked his old-fashioned style, though it clashed with the austerity of the modern accommodations.

"Sign here."

I signed there.

He took back the pen and wrote a number three on the line with my name.

He handed me a key. It read, *Do not copy* on the head. The key ring had a brass coin stamped with a *3*. He said, "It's in the middle."

I thanked him, and we wished each other a good night. I went, again, out into the cold.

And not for the last time that night.

The room was definitely worth the whole twenty. And then some. There was a bed, a bathroom, and a door that locked—I locked it—plus a small writing desk with a small pad of paper and small lamp that lit when I flipped the wall switch. No television.

I pulled the chair out from the desk and set it underneath the door handle, tilted back against the door. It probably wouldn't stop a determined intruder, but it might slow him down.

I wasn't paranoid, but someone had already gotten the drop on me once today by the car thief, and I was not hoping for a second helping, especially with him being snowed in too. He might panic and realize I was around and able to identify him. Except I couldn't remember him—just his height and the vague features distorted by his injuries.

I undressed and turned on the shower as hot as it would go. Steam filled the bathroom, like a sauna. I waited on the tile until feeling returned to my extremities before turning the shower from scalding to just hot. Stepping into the rush of water, I felt instantly better. My headache had subsided.

After a long and thoughtful while, I turned off the shower and dried myself with decent towels, not the usual tissue-thin ones in most no-name inns. Maybe no TV sets meant better everything else.

Upon further investigation I saw just how far my money stretched. In a plastic cup was a toothbrush heat-sealed in cellophane. I'd trade a TV for a toothbrush anytime. I cleaned my teeth and looked over my wound in the mirror. It was not terrible. I wouldn't be appearing in any fashion magazines anytime soon, but I was no Quasimodo.

Then came the unpleasant part. I put my cold, sodden clothes back on. Then, pocketing the toothbrush, I switched off the light and moved the chair back to its original place. I left the door unlocked and walked back to the office. The lights were dim, but the door was still unlocked. It was only a couple of hours before midnight, and I hoped the nice man was fast asleep. I didn't want to bother him again.

I slipped behind the counter, checking the key rack. Numbers 15 and 11 were gone. From the way the motel was laid out, I gathered those rooms were upstairs. Maybe their occupants were hoping for a better view of that big Montana sky when the snow cleared. Or maybe they just liked being high up. Heat rises, after all. I took number two and replaced it with my number three key. I didn't think the car thief would come after me, but if he did, he might check the register and all the rooms. That was a good reason to go with the ground floor. It would be a lot easier to escape out of a window.

Once in my new suite I did the chair-against-the-door thing and showered again, for good measure. I cranked up the heater and laid all my clothes across it to dry. Then I set out the contents of my pockets on the writing desk.

There wasn't much—just my room key, my passport, and a fold of bills, with the new addition of the toothbrush. Of course, there was a brand-new toothbrush in this room as well, but I didn't want to defraud an innkeeper by taking two toothbrushes.

I was one hundred percent spent. I sank to my knees on the low-pile carpet and said a prayer, thanking God for keeping me and prospering me for one more day. My head had barely touched the pillow before I was in a deep, deep sleep.

I didn't know what time it was when I woke up. I felt well-rested, so I must have slept for about the recommended amount. But I didn't know when I had gone to bed either. I don't wear a watch. The motel didn't supply those brick-sized alarm clocks with the angry red numbers.

Not that I needed to know the time. I had nowhere to go, no pressing appointments.

I rolled out from under the covers and back to my knees, praying for a good day, which I entirely expected. My face no longer hurt. The bump on my head was still solid but manageable.

I showered again, just to warm up. I had neglected soap the night before. Usually motels begrudgingly issue a sliver of solidified dish detergent wrapped in waxy paper, which you use in one go, but I was rewarded for having to make do without an alarm clock and television with a big bar of lavender-scented soap. There were also miniature bottles of brand-name shampoo and conditioner, not the liquid dish detergent you find elsewhere.

I redressed, wishing I could keep my clothes as warm as they were from right off the heater. It is the little things that make you feel good, like cozy clothes and hot water. For the last two years I had been living in places where the only hot water was what you boiled on a stove or over a fire. Sometimes we didn't have running water and had to shower in the rain.

My clothes were new and durable. New to me, that is. I had bought them secondhand because I figured they had already lasted long enough for someone else—Why not me?—and because buying brand-new clothes was among the greatest ways to waste money.

Fifty dollars for a T-shirt? No, thank you.

The walkway to the office was sheltered by a sloped roof, but a thin layer of snow had blown in sideways. I left footprints along the walk, which I hoped would soon be masked with more drifting.

I stepped inside. The guy was in his office with the door open. He was in a big recliner, reading. Seeing me, he set down his book and began to stand.

"Don't bother getting up, sir. I'm not checking out."

He sighed gratefully, easing back down, like maybe pain from an old injury was exacerbated by the cold. "Staying another night?"

"Yes, I believe I will." I examined my cash roll, came up with four fives, and set them on the counter.

The guy nodded and resumed reading.

"Got the time?"

His eyes flicked up. There must have been a clock above the doorway inside the office.

"Quarter to nine."

"Know a place to buy a coat?"

"Trapper's, just on the other side of Main Street. Gas station is there too." He pointed.

"Thanks."

I knew Main Street to be the twelve o'clock spoke, so the other side of it would put the general store on the one o'clock. Outside was warmer than it had been at night. A couple of cars slewed by. I would hold off on the coat until after breakfast. A school bus full of little kids drove by, undeterred by the weather, all of its passengers looking like arctic explorers in big puffy coats and hats and mittens. I trudged through the snow, churning the fresh white into dirty slush. I saw not-quite-even rows of neat, cozy houses, with plenty of snow-filled space between them and smoke rising from chimneys. Christmas lights were strung all over. Folks were shoveling driveways. Just like in a postcard.

The gray-white of the sky merged perfectly with the gray-white ground, with the faint seam of mountains and evergreens running along the length of the horizon.

The coat could wait. I was hungry, like a bear out of hibernation.

Half a dozen cars lined the front of the Oak Table, like horses at a trough.

I was expecting a lot of hubbub and noise—the morning crowd, regulars chatting up the pretty redheaded waitress.

I was wrong. Being wrong seemed to be a bad habit for me lately.

Inside everyone was silent. They were all at different tables but huddled in a loose group, looking at the television set. Mary and another waitress stood side by side, slightly behind the patrons, their attention also rapt. I skirted the please-wait-to-be-seated sign and made my way over to Mary.

Images on the screen showed what the news ticker scrolling across the bottom of the screen was calling *Snowpocalypse.* The highway patrol had closed many of the main arteries, and downed trees and snow had left other routes impassable. Schools across the western part of the state were closing. Clearly Cluff hadn't gotten the memo.

A lot of Christmas travels were interrupted, and collisions had resulted in serious injuries. At least another foot of new powder was expected in less than a week, and visibility would be reduced to close to zero on the roads. Massive power outages were projected. Citizens were advised to stay indoors and ration food and fuel because stores were expected to be running low on supplies for at least a few days.

I watched and listened out of respect for the room and because I always aim for empathy. But I was mildly surprised at the reverence. I was mostly out of the loop as far as current events go. Maybe a new trend of solemnity during the morning news was sweeping the nation. Or at least Cluff, Montana. Maybe everyone was expecting relatives from out of town who would be late or not coming at all. Maybe they were all thinking about filling up their tubs with water, gassing up generators, and replenishing their woodboxes.

But news is news. Sometimes it was good, sometimes it wasn't. Storms happen all the time. And as troublesome as inclement weather can be, it rarely merits letting your hash browns get cold. I looked a question at Mary, and she leaned in close. I smelled coconut shampoo and maple syrup.

"This is a small town, obviously; people are worried about what the bad weather is going to do when it gets here."

I pointed outside. "What do you call this?"

"This is nothing."

My spot in the corner from the night before was taken, so I moved to sit at a different table. There was news about some overturned semitrucks. A spokesperson was droning on about *no details at this time.* Sitting down sideways on the bench, I caught Mary's eye. She patted the air with her hand and held up her index finger.

Wait right there; I'll be just a minute.

As I waited, a lot of questions about time and space and police procedure were incubating in my head. I felt a little guilty being glad for the weather that was worrying everyone, since it had waylaid the murderer too. My car's tank had been full enough to have gotten him out of the state if it hadn't been for the snow.

Mary was on her way to me when the door opened.

This time I looked. I had been facing the television, so my relative angle to the entryway was poor. I turned to the entrance, and as I did, I first caught a glimpse out the window and saw a Cluff Police Department SUV.

Not good.

Rock and French sauntered in, cool as cucumbers. They disregarded the sign to wait to be seated. But then again, so had I.

They were in uniform.

They saw me and smirked, brushing their hands on their guns like they were dusting the butts off.

For the past two years, as a missionary in Peru, I had had it pretty good.

Not too many people tried to mess with me, maybe because I am a lot bigger than most people there. But I am also white, and to many Peruvians, that is synonymous with money. Here and there we would get a few drunks who'd spit in our faces, but that was the worst of it for me. Until one day, some punk had approached my fellow missionary and me on a dark street at night and pulled a short-barreled revolver on us. He'd told us he had a weapon, which was superfluous because we saw it.

I had been all set to clamp a hand on the gun's frame to stop the hammer from moving. I had rehearsed in my mind jerking the gun around and breaking the robber's trigger finger in the process, which I had planned on following up with a straight right to his solar plexus and an elbow to the temple. But then that still, soft voice asked me rhetorically, *What would Jesus do?*, which I thought was exceptionally inconvenient.

So my companion and I had looked at one another and smiled, and I held up the softcover set of scriptures I carried everywhere and said, "We have a weapon too. It's called the Book of Mormon. Ever heard of it?"

The guy with the gun must have figured we were downright crazy because he decided right then and there to drop the whole armed-robbery angle. Or maybe his shoulder angel got to him. We would see him around town from time to time after that, and he would nod and pass by.

But now I was facing the potential of two guns in the hands of two guys who didn't like me. And I wasn't armed with the word of God. I'd left my scriptures in the Buick. I didn't expect the carjacker to have read very far in them or to have marked his favorite passages.

I was comfortable disarming someone who had a gun right up in my face or against my head, but Rock and French were out of reach. Besides, if I did that, I would have to go all the way and break some bones, and I was not yet prepared to burn my bridge with Strawn.

I had information for the chief, and he was keeping me out of jail. And it would do me no good at all to be on the run in a small town I didn't know and couldn't leave.

But just because I was unwilling to fight Strawn's goons then and there didn't mean I was unwilling to run.

Fight or flight. The oldest, most significant binary decision in the world, after right or wrong, of course, but that is more a pattern of belief and practice than a recurring choice.

They saw that they had my attention, unlike the night before. Their smiles spread, and they stepped farther into the dining room. Rock motioned for me to go to the back of the room. I did not want them behind me, so I responded with a gesture that said, *No, after you.*

CHAPTER FIVE

THEY DIDN'T WANT TO STAND there and argue, so they moved on and I followed, a little warily. I believed most men and women in uniform were good people. But by no means were all of them. People automatically saw cops as beacons of wisdom and honor, which wasn't always true. They can be just as bad as anyone else. The jury was still out on these two. Other than a little disparagement, I hadn't done anything to merit their dislike, as far as I knew. Maybe they were just naturally surly. At least there were witnesses now, in case they wanted to rumble.

We sat down. Just like the night before.

"Can I help you?" I asked.

"Sawyer, right?" Rock said.

He obviously already knew the answer to that. Strawn must have told them, because French hadn't asked my name when he arrested me.

"That's right," I said.

"Why are you here?" Rock asked, just like the night before. I looked from Rock to French and then back again. "You know why I'm here."

Rock clicked his tongue. "No, besides the snow-in and the accident."

Collision, I mentally corrected.

He continued. "Why are you in Cluff at all? We're not a tourist town, not in winter anyway. We're not on the road to anywhere."

I kept my hands on the table and leaned back. "I heard it was a nice town, and thanks for the big welcome."

"We're just saying we don't like you," Rock said.

"Good to know," I said.

"So you need to get lost," Rock said, jabbing his finger in my direction. I wanted to tell them then and there that as soon as I could, I would be gone forever. I'd never call, never write, never even look back. But I didn't want them to have that satisfaction. I don't like being told what to do.

"I will leave when I am good and ready. Speaking of which, you guys find my car yet?"

Rock glared. "No."

"Well, you find my car, you find the guy, you'll be heroes, and I'll be gone."

They mulled over the idea. *Heroes. Me gone. Doing their actual jobs instead of playing patty cake or whatever it was they did all day.*

Then they chose a different route.

Rock reached to his belt and pulled out a pair of handcuffs. "Or we could just detain you until this mystery man shows up."

I narrowed my eyes and pulled my hands down to my lap.

Rock kept talking. "We've had problems in this town with strange drifters in the past, and you're a suspicious dude."

To be fair, I was. All I had was the clothes on my back and what was in my pockets. I had no fixed address, no cellphone, and no references I could easily reach.

Not good.

The thought of jail did not appeal to me. All my life I had done and gone as I pleased. Even with the strict missionary schedule, I had been free to walk around and sleep on rooftops on particularly hot jungle nights and see a whole new set of constellations.

Being in a cinderblock box would bring me as close to being afraid as I could imagine, claustrophobia at its finest.

So I was a little desperate.

French leaned around to see the rest of the room. Everyone was done with the news and had returned to their breakfast.

Mary came by with a mug of hot chocolate for me without even having been asked. She already knew me so well, after barely having spoken with me. She asked French and Rock if they wanted anything. They said no. Someone called for a refill of coffee. Rock and French watched Mary walk away and then turned back to me.

Rock continued. "So, Sawyer, we can do this the easy way or the fun way. My vote is the fun way, but it's up to you."

I was afraid of nothing. But I could end up charged with murder. This was a small town, and I didn't foresee any kind of a fair trial. Maybe some excessive force from Rock. I had gotten off very easy the first time around, and the circumstances surrounding the dead guy were too strange to let a loose end like me off. Maybe the FBI would demand a scapegoat. The Cluff PD would have to cede to the bureau.

I didn't know how much I could rely on Strawn a second time. Actually I knew *exactly* how much I could rely on Strawn, or anyone else for that matter—not at all. I could only count on myself.

Fine by me.

Rock grinned and looked expectantly at me. "Well? What's it going to be? Easy way or fun way?"

How about both, moron? Fun and easy. For me.

I tried to look complacent and deflated, nonthreatening. I raised my hands slowly, like I was surrendering. Then, before my hands came all the way up, I knocked over my hot cocoa. They yelped in surprise, leaning away from the oncoming tidal wave of molten chocolate. French looked severely dismayed, like he might melt on contact. Rock looked like he was worried about staining his uniform.

Then I broke George Washington's fourteenth rule: "Jog not the table on which another reads or writes."

The tables in back were not bolted to the floor; they were free to move and combine for large parties or maybe to clear the floor for dancing or live music or whatever. So I put both hands on the edge and shoved hard. They had been in the process of standing up to avoid the spill, so the table hit them down low, forcing them back into their chairs. I kept pushing and pinned them with the table.

Then I ran, hitting tables and chairs aside and dodging the folks who were now upset by two things: the news about the impending bad weather and the strange young man making a big mess.

I would have to apologize to Mary and the other waitress.

The cops yelled, and I burst through the batwing doors into the kitchen. A curly haired, jolly-looking grill man stared up in surprise, holding on to his spatula like it was a life preserver. I vaulted boxes of foodstuffs and out the door into a fenced area with a dumpster and grease receptacle. I took a running jump and landed on the closed lid of the dumpster. Placing my palms on the top of the wooden fence, I lifted myself up and swung my legs around, pivoting on my hands. I landed and rolled in the snow.

Straightening up, I waited, listening for just a second, to see if I would get lucky. I did.

Both Rock and French came barreling out through the kitchen door, shouting. Just one or neither of them would have been a problem.

If they had been smart, they would have gone straight back to their vehicle and chased me in heated, four-wheel-drive comfort. If they had been *really* smart, one would have gone back to the SUV, and one would have followed on foot.

But they were not really smart. Maybe they were just barely smarter than the average bear as well, but not a smidgen more. I ran around to the front of the Oak Table and hopped right into the driver's seat of their SUV, easy as you please.

Bingo.

They had left it unlocked and idling. That way they wouldn't have to have the keys jangling on their belts. And it was a safety concern. Police have to be able to get in and go in a hurry. If they hadn't kept the heat on, they would have come out to an iced-up windshield, and then they'd have to scrape it. And who in their right mind would steal a police car anyway?

I figured while I was busy committing aggravated assault on a peace officer, I might as well add grand theft auto and felony evasion to the list.

It was clear Rock had driven. I had to rack the seat forward. Then I hit the gas, rolling out of the parking lot.

I buckled up for safety. It's the law.

Without much thought I turned down random side streets, trying to put distance between me and the cops. I opted for an overall counterclockwise route. I remembered the general layout from the map.

The roads were still covered in snow, and worn tracks like wagon wheel ruts provided the only viable path. A couple of people who were out and about waved at me. I waved back. They must not have recognized me as a stranger through the tinted glass.

Rock and French had proved how smart they weren't. Next I waited to see how scared they were. I hoped they would be too afraid to get on the radio and call for backup. They would never live it down. They might even lose their jobs.

I figured I could launch my own investigation and find the real bad guy. Maybe Strawn would forgive me for smacking his deputies around and stealing police property.

I realized, though, that I might have just jumped out of the frying pan and into the fire. Or whatever the frozen variation was for the expression. *Out of the pond and into the freezer?* In my efforts to avoid possible jail time, I might have just guaranteed it.

But whatever.

I was free for the moment, and that was good enough. For now.

When I was a kid, I never planned anything, never made lists, never even had a calendar. My dad used to say I was "flying by the seat of my pants." To which I would invariably reply, "Yeah, but I'm *flying*."

Things hadn't changed much.

The first time I'd gotten suspended for fighting was in high school. It had been the result of a spur-of-the-moment, gut-feeling, knee-jerk reaction, like stealing the car had been.

I had been outside during lunch, not eating, just standing around talking. I had seen a big kid grab a new guy by the shirt front and dump chocolate milk on his head, and I didn't think. Not one bit. I can barely remember moving, but I'd pushed the bully back to separate him from the new guy and knocked him down with a right hook.

I'd gotten kicked out for three days and had to forfeit a swim meet. I thought my father would be angry, but he wasn't. We'd gotten takeout and watched action movies. It was probably one of the best times of my life.

I did not expect a similar happy outcome with my most recent rash decision.

But, then again, there is a saying that fortune favors the bold. It was a Latin proverb adopted by the United States Marine Corps. I might have added *sometimes* to the motto.

Rolling through a four-way stop, I checked my mirrors. No pursuit, for now.

Driving the big SUV was a lot different than driving the Buick. I liked it. Enough maybe to have taken it out of town if I could have. It's not like I was very busy at the moment.

Continuing along no-name roads, I hit dead-ends at the eight and seven o'clock spokes before I made it to the six o'clock, which was just a continuation of Main Street. There were no traffic lights, just occasional stop signs.

I maneuvered back around the town, hoping to make at least one full circuit. I switched between the inner and outer rings to avoid the center. I figured as long as I had a set of wheels on loan, I would see what there was to see.

Which wasn't much.

Cluff was just a regular town. It had everything it needed and nothing it didn't. Trappers, the place the innkeeper had told me about, was in the middle of a wide patch of snow. Once upon a time, it might have been a parking lot. It looked like the mom-and-pop general store I had hoped to see last night. It would have been just a bit too brazen for my taste to stop to shop just then, so I passed the store and the gas station opposite it.

Further down the road I saw an auto repair shop. A large hand-painted sign said they repaired all models. Including Buick

Skylarks, I hoped. Once I got my car back I would bring it in. The bay doors were closed against the cold, but I could see a couple of people inside.

I turned around, taking the outer ring, this time clockwise. At the end of the two o'clock spoke I saw a schoolyard. It seemed to be an all-inclusive campus, K–12, and was divided up between a big main building and scattered portables.

Recess was in session. A handful of kids, defiant to the cold, were playing on a wooden jungle gym.

I like kids. There is something so innately good about children; it's no wonder Christ commands us to become like them. I wondered what the kids I had met in Peru would have thought if they could have seen snow. The youngest son of a family we had baptized had taken an hour to be persuaded to step into the font waters. He had cried and recoiled at every encouraging word or gesture from his family and from us. He'd said it was much too cold. Clearly he had never been to Cluff. Finally, he had worked up the courage.

Sometimes we would use electric water-heating pitchers people use to make tea and dump them into the font. But the pitchers were so small they never made a difference.

One time, in the jungle, there was a period of about two weeks when the temperature dropped from more than ninety degrees and sunny to fifty degrees and overcast. It reminded me a lot of the Pacific Northwest and was a bit of a relief. My Guatemalan companion had worn a knitted sweater the whole time. Usually all people wore there were thin, sleeveless shirts, shorts, and sandals or no shoes at all. They had not taken the change well.

I didn't see much else. The initial high of escape was wearing off.

I was running out of places to go, and I couldn't hide forever. Not having a lot of options is about the same thing as having too many.

Just keep driving.

That was all I could do. But for how much longer, I didn't know. Pretty soon I would end up driving in circles. Or out of gas. The gauge was low. The houses became more sparse and the trees thicker. I was nearing the east edge of town. The three o'clock spoke. At the end of the spokes the roads just fizzled out into nothing. Just trees and snow.

Strawn would know by now and no doubt regretted his clemency. The radio was silent, so they must have been communicating by cell phone.

The only way I could see to vindicate myself was to break the case on my own. I backed up, drove forward, backed up again, and so on until I had turned around. I took the next side street I came to.

Topping a rise, I saw what looked like a sheep farm. But it was hard to tell just from off-white shapes on a more-white backdrop. I looked out across the white expanse.

People say Montana is "big sky country," which was true, in that it was big. But it was not wide and open and free. Not at the moment. With the low cloud layer, it looked long and hard and bleak, like an ocean of concrete.

I had taken the four o'clock spoke all the way to the end when I stopped driving.

The snow was piled high, like a miniature avalanche had happened there. I wondered if that was how the highway looked and knew it would take a whole lot of snowplows or some extreme heat wave to get through it before spring. I was about to begin the long process of turning around again when I saw something. On the left side of the road, barely visible, was a flash of red. Bumping the gear shift into park, I flung the door open and spilled out.

I didn't look both ways crossing the street—an inadvisable choice—but there was still no traffic. And I was sure I had just seen my Buick.

Sinking into the snow, I saw two things at once: The farm was definitely for sheep. There were a few gathering at an old split-rail fence. And it was definitely my Buick, mostly hidden beneath the low limbs of the trees and with a heavy coat of snow. It must have been there at least all morning and probably since last night.

It looked to be sound. Besides the sundry superficial scrapes from the crash, there was no other damage. The doors were locked, which had been very conscientious of the car thief. He must have been planning on coming back for it. Maybe. It was a distinctive car and therefore easily identified.

I hadn't thought to see the Buick again so soon. It was pretty much a miracle. The thief must have been pretty disappointed when he'd hit the east end of town and seen it snowed in too. He must have turned around and found the nearest spot to stash it.

I wondered where he could be now. Not outside. Not in this weather. Maybe he was hiding in a barn. With the sheep. Wool and hay would keep him warm.

Reaching up and under the rear fender, I fished out the key hidden in a little black box with twin magnetic strips on the back. The older I get the more prepared I need to be, so I kept a spare.

She started fine, but the snow was deep and I could barely back her an inch before bogging down. Police cars usually have a lot of supplies in them—odds and ends for emergencies—so I turned off the Buick and checked the SUV. There was plenty of stuff in the back of Rock's rig: all the usual things like first-aid, road flares, reflective vests, tow cables, emergency blankets, rock salt, snow chains, and jumper cables. And there was an axe. It was not the typical roadside assistance gear, but it was just right for the back of beyond in the Montana wilderness.

I took a look at the axe. It was a handsome item manufactured by the Hudson Bay Company, one of the longest-running operations in the western world. I'm a fan of westerns and cowboy movies, but I think the real iconic American frontiersmen were the mountain men. Solitary wanderers. Stoics, surviving in the simplest of ways and by the purest of means. They were exactly what I wanted to be.

The axe was slightly lighter and smaller than what one might find in Granddad's woodshed. The blade was keen and more angular than rounded.

The head was flawless and shiny—not a scratch on it—so I figured the cops didn't use it much and, therefore, it would not be missed.

I cut a few boughs off nearby trees, laying them beneath the wheels of my Buick and all the way to the road. They provided just enough traction, and soon I was right back where I had been yesterday: on the road, in my own car.

Except I was going back to town. I had no other choice. I put the axe on the floor behind the passenger seat, where I could reach it easily from where I sat. It might come in handy again. I breathed in and out. I'd left the cop car idling so it would be warm when they finally found it, which couldn't take too terribly long.

And it didn't. Because at that moment a big crew cab pickup truck with Cluff PD decals and flashing lights trundled over the hill, turning lengthwise across the road, blocking me.

I had nowhere to go.

This vehicle was a lot more up-to-date than either Rock's or French's. There were more lights, there were bigger rails, and there was a brush guard on the front that looked like it would serve as a battering ram. I could see stainless side-boxes, probably full of whatever a rural first responder might need. The wheels looked like they could have handled any terrain. The frame was jacked up to accommodate the heavy-duty tires. It was probably complete with aftermarket suspension and supercharged. There were twin spotlights on either side of the windshield posts. All the bells and whistles.

A cop I hadn't met before stepped out, gun in hand.

Not again.

This guy looked to be a shade older than Strawn. He was tall and lean, like a middleweight boxer, just slightly lighter than what I had competed at. His hair was platinum white and cropped brutally short.

He looked like he knew what he was doing—sure of himself. There was no twitching or shaking of the gun. The barrel was rock steady. I could have sworn he was going to shoot me. Then I recognized him from the hunting photograph on his desk, remembered the dead deer.

I put my hands up.

"Get out of the car," he barked.

I did so. Slowly. But I stood by the door.

"I'm unarmed," I said.

"I've got two APBs out, one for that red car and one for a police vehicle," the guy said.

"Well, I couldn't be driving both, now, could I?" I said.

"You being smart with me?" he asked, aiming a little more carefully.

"No, sir. Just pointing out things you might have to think about later."

Snow started again, instantly falling full throttle, not the slow start that builds up over time.

And then another police truck came rolling down upon our standoff. Chief Strawn stepped out from the driver's side. He was out of uniform, in a plain-blue denim button-up over a white T-shirt. Rock burst from the passenger side; he looked to have a pretty good grouch on.

CHAPTER SIX

I WAS GLAD I WAS already out of the car. I figured there was not much worse than being stuck in a car with armed men all around. Of course, your best option is to run them over. But I couldn't get through the truck. And, except in extreme cases, vehicular manslaughter is not the right choice.

And only one of the three had a weapon in hand, which was encouraging. But there were three of them, which wasn't.

One guy is nothing, and two is not much more of a problem. But three presents a lot of variables that make a successful hand-to-hand encounter tougher, even if you can keep them all in front of so you can't be attacked from behind like I had been the previous day. Three is a perfect storm. More than that, and they can all get in each other's way so you can skirt around and line them up before picking them off one at a time, like ducks in a shooting gallery. And, usually, once a couple of heads have been acquainted with the pavement, the rest come to the conclusion that they should just cut their losses and run. But three guys can come at you all at once and from multiple sides.

Of course, all things aside, running is usually the most sustainable choice.

Fight or flight.

Some people say the best fights are the ones you never have. I disagree. The best fights are the ones you win quickly and decisively, without a scratch except for those on your knuckles.

Keeping the open door between me and the cops, I ran through my mental database of past fights. Not the sanctioned bouts in a ring, with referees and rules.

No, I was recalling the real ones. The ones without breaks every few minutes, when I was just as likely to get killed as not.

When I was nine, on a playground a lot like the one I had seen earlier in Cluff, I fought my first fight. That had been against two twelve-year-olds, and I had put them down hard. And they'd deserved it. They should have known better than to steal money from my little sister's lemonade stand.

In all of my hard-won battles I had never faced three at once. Not yet.

And all three of the men before me were above average—in terms of size, that is, and probably strength. And I could safely assume all three had extensive training in defensive tactics from the academy.

I closed the door and stepped around to the hood. The cops congregated into a loose semicircle around me, well out of reach.

Strawn was in the center, flanked by his deputies. The white-haired guy faded to my left, keeping me in the line of fire without putting his partners in the way. Rock assumed a posture that was somewhere between a boxing stance and that of a linebacker before the snap.

Strawn spoke, holding up his hands reassuringly. "I see you found your car. Nice ride."

The tension was broken. They weren't looking for a fight. Strawn shook his head once at Rock and motioned to the other guy by chopping his hand sideways through the air in slow motion, like he was an umpire signaling *safe* with one hand.

The cop I hadn't seen before holstered his weapon.

Rock just stood there frowning, maybe mad I wasn't in cuffs on the ground yet.

I said nothing.

Strawn did the whole rueful awe-shucks-I-don't-want-to-bring-it-up-but-I-gotta thing, like the good old boy he was. He rubbed the back of his neck. "Well, Mr. Sawyer, there is the little issue of your . . . uh . . . procurement of a police vehicle."

I shrugged. "I don't need it anymore, and it saved your department having to look for my car."

He rolled his jaw.

The cop I didn't know looked like he wanted to say something but didn't.

Strawn turned back to his truck. "Let's get out of the snow. We don't mind so much, but I'm sure you're not used to it, and you've got no coat."

"The bad guy is probably close; I found the car right there," I said, pointing back the way I had come.

Strawn looked contemplative and then pointed at Rock and the other guy. "Rock, call French. You two check the outbuildings around here. Knock on some doors. Lang, back on patrol. Mr. Sawyer, if you'll follow me to my office." The chief spoke evenly— no barking orders. He was just a guy who said things, and then they happened.

I said nothing—just climbed back into my car.

He nodded, and I waited until Strawn turned and inched up the hill. Then I followed, leaving Rock and Lang to turn the SUV around. I was glad Strawn had sent the other two off on other errands. He seemed like an okay guy, torn between his good nature and the exigencies of the job.

I felt a brief but very big jolt as I entered the lobby. What if they had duped me into a false sense of security? I imagined Strawn didn't want to make a big chase all across town; he could lure me back to the station all on my own and toss me in the clink before throwing away the keys. But I did not think he would have sent his boys away if that had been their scheme.

Strawn was already inside, stoking the fireplace; he had removed his overshirt. "Mr. Sawyer."

He extended his hand again, and I shook it. I noticed his knotted forearms were as big as my calves. I hoped I never had to arm wrestle him.

I decided to accept his friendliness at face value. "How are you, Chief?"

He smiled guilelessly. "I'll be better when this business is behind us. At least you got your vehicle back."

"I'd trade all the cars in the world to bring back the dead guy," I said.

"Life is a kick in the teeth, and then you die. Bad situation all around. But we'll find the perp, make no mistake. He can't be far. I'm sorry if you thought I doubted your story at all." Strawn clapped a hand on my shoulder. It was heavy. My knees nearly buckled. "That is what we wanted to talk to you about, before you took off."

"Your boys looked like they might shoot first and ask questions never."

Strawn missed barely a beat and then recovered. "It seems you all got off on the wrong foot. No more independent action from you though. Let us handle this. I will keep them off your case."

I had been hopeful enough that I would avoid arrest but had been sure I would get a long lecture. But he didn't even bat an eye. Hadn't even mentioned me hitting his deputies with the table, which was beyond surprising. But, regardless of his reasons, I wasn't complaining.

"Thanks for that. And thanks for not minding about the joyride."

He smiled under his moustache. "At least you didn't crash that one. Or let it get stolen." Strawn motioned me back into his office with a jerk of his head. "Well, Mr. Sawyer, you may have heard we are due for some worse weather."

I nodded. "I was in the café when the news announced it. People were pretty worried about the storm."

"Actually two storms. One from the west and one from the northeast. We're going to be the meat in a snow sandwich. And if those folks knew a poor bullet-riddled body was tossed right outside of town, they'd be beside themselves." I nodded, and he continued. "So, I want you to keep what you know quiet, just until we get a read on the situation."

I understood. It was one thing for the town to find out a storm was coming but another to know there was a murderer in their midst.

A matter of disclosure.

"I can do that," I said.

He smiled, apparently relieved I didn't need more convincing. But I did. At least in one respect.

"What about the body?"

"We can't get out there until the roads clear. That's the bottom line. There's no way. But the conditions are ideal for preservation, and we aren't worried about critters."

"Have you called the FBI?" I asked.

"And tell them what? That we may or may not have one of theirs frozen stiff in the snow, with no leads, one witness, and a snowed-in town? They couldn't do anything until the storm passes anyway, not even land a helicopter."

I understood. Sort of. It was what some people called compartmentalization. Timing was vital. And maybe he wanted to save a little face and have a prisoner to show the feds when they finally came. It would be embarrassing if Strawn couldn't find the needle in his fairly small, snowed-in haystack.

Strawn waited for me to comment and continued when I didn't. "The town's doctor doubles as our examiner and will perform the autopsy, unless the feds want to wait even longer to do so themselves. Good thing you threw a monkey wrench into the perp's plans. We might never have known what happened."

That brought up another question.

"Why do you think he was driving with a dead guy? He could have tossed him out anywhere."

"Maybe he had a spot in mind for disposal."

A cell phone rang, a high-pitched, generic trill. Strawn pulled the little rectangle from his breast pocket, looked at it, and must have hit a button to ignore it. He stood up. "Well, thank you, Mr. Sawyer, for your cooperation. The whole department is looking for that son of a gun. Thanks to your description, it shouldn't be long before we find him."

That didn't make a whole lot of sense to me. I hadn't provided a detailed portrait. The guy was nondescript, average everything. He had no tattoos, no distinguishing marks, besides the bumps from the crash. I had not even taken a good look at him. The only thing that might have identified him had been my car, which I had found. My coat, too, unless he had ditched it.

"Was that French?" I asked, pantomiming a phone call.

His forehead creased. "As a matter of fact, yes, it was. He's probably reporting on an assignment I sent him on. We couldn't all go hunting you down. Speaking of which, what is your room number? In case we need to get a statement?"

"Three," I said.

I wanted to ask more questions but couldn't articulate them at the moment. So Strawn walked me back out to the lobby. I pushed through the double doors, entirely unsatisfied.

I am curious by nature. And stubborn.

I realized I was also hungry. It was almost lunchtime, and I hadn't even had breakfast. I was facing an energy crisis. It was not a good habit to start, but it was certainly rectifiable.

I drove to the restaurant through the life-size snow globe. It was a much more enjoyable trip than last night's frozen hike. I didn't see Rock or French or Lang, which was fine with me. I could go the rest of my life without seeing them, and I would have counted it among the greatest of blessings. I felt I had struck out in the friends department with all three deputies and was on thin ice with Strawn.

The parking lot was a little sparser when I got there and the snow a lot thicker. Maybe people were already beating hasty retreats to their burrows.

I parked and pocketed the spare key. I made sure the car was locked.

Mary was gone when I got back to the restaurant. So were all the previous patrons. Some newcomers were scattered about, but nobody who had seen my desperate flight from the law. Except the other waitress.

She came out from the kitchen with a pot of coffee. She looked distressed. When she saw me, she stopped. Putting a hand on a hip, she grilled me with a glare.

"Are you going to run all over the place again, or are you going to sit and eat like a normal person?"

I inclined my head in an abbreviated bow. "Ma'am, I am sorry for the trouble. I know you and Mary had to clean up my mess. I'm just here to eat. Anyway, I couldn't run much farther on an empty stomach."

With a tilt of her head in acknowledgment of my promise, she went around refilling coffee.

The corner table I had sat at last night was open again, so I took it.

Without being asked, the waitress set a mug of cocoa in front of me, just like Mary had done.

"Try not to spill this one," she said.

I thanked her, but she was already vanishing back into the kitchen. A handful of people came through the door. This seemed to be the lunch-hour rush, such as it was. I didn't want to put the waitress out any more than I already had, so I held off on my order.

Breakfast and lunch are my standardized meals. Everywhere I go I get some variation of pancakes, bacon, and eggs in the mornings and a sandwich for lunch, preferably corned beef, though I sometimes settle for pastrami. I tend to vary on dinners, but any of the aforementioned edibles are always plausible candidates.

They don't make pancakes or sandwiches in Peru, so I had a lot of catching up to do.

Letting my cocoa cool and the other lunchers order ahead of me, I followed a sign to the restrooms and washed up.

I came back and found the waitress sitting at my table. Maybe that was a Montana thing. I wasn't complaining.

I sat down. She looked at me. I sipped my cocoa—perfect temperature.

"Mary said you're all right."

I swallowed and smiled, looking down. "That is a very generous estimation."

"You seem all right."

"Thank you. You're kind," I said.

She was taller than average, with curly auburn hair, graying on the ends. She wore it shorter than most, like she was more concerned with getting out the door in the morning. But it looked good on her. She had sharp, appraising features that made her look like a very pretty bird of prey. She was lined almost equally by smiles and worry, and she was tan, but not from the sun, not in this season—just naturally olive-toned.

"I'm Agnes Kirk. This is my establishment."

"I'm sorry," I said.

"You're sorry?"

"I mean, I'm Sawyer; my name is Sawyer. I meant I'm sorry for the trouble I caused you earlier."

She waved that off. "No harm, no foul; I'll just charge you for a broken mug. But I'm always happy to see someone stick it to the police."

"Why is that?"

"Mary said you're nice to talk to."

I was really hungry, but it would have been rude to order right then. *Oh, it's nice to meet you, and thanks for the compliment. Now, how about you make me a sandwich with a couple of pickles on the side.*

"So is she," I said. "You don't like the police?"

"Not *those* policemen," she said.

"Why?"

She sighed. "That is a very long story, and I have some more work to do. Mary will be back soon; she was hoping you'd be back."

"Pardon my saying so, ma'am, but it isn't often you see a business owner bussing tables."

"Are you a restaurateur, Mr. Sawyer?"

"No," I said. "But I'm a human being on planet earth. Are you short-staffed or something?"

She stood up. "No. At least, I wasn't until today, which is what Mary and I were going to talk to you about. She'll be back in a couple of hours. Will you wait?"

For Mary? You bet, I thought. I nodded.

"Can I get something started for you? To eat, that is. Anything with Mary you'll have to arrange yourself." She winked at me, which made me blush.

I asked for a Reuben sandwich. She said that was a good choice and went off to check on other patrons.

I wondered what it was they wanted to talk to me about. It certainly couldn't be a job. I wasn't planning on sticking around long enough to fill out any kind of forms or learn customers' names and usual orders.

So I sat and waited and thought. It felt good to have reclaimed my car. My work here was done. Except it wasn't, not really, mostly because the roads were closed and partly because I don't like being beaten. I'm not exceptionally competitive or vengeful or anything. I really didn't care that the guy had bushwhacked me and made off with my car. Those were occupational hazards for incorrigible Good Samaritans. No good deed goes unpunished and all that. So I didn't mind that so much. Actually it had been kind of a wake-up call. I needed to be more vigilant, hyperaware of any and all situations.

No, what bothered me was that I had been an arms' length away from a cold-blooded killer, and I had let him get away.

When I was in Peru, I was serving in an area for several months, and in the local congregation was a middle-aged guy from Holland who would share his incoherent "testimony" over the pulpit every month in broken Spanish. His name was Peter. He was the only member there who could play the piano, and he did so exceptionally well. But he was a little off, with a wild-eyed look and a scraggly ring of long blond hair haloing a bulbous bald head. His veins throbbed in his temples, and he was always in need of spare food, clothing, and money.

We were always cordial and helpful, brotherly. He lived in the bishop's spare room, selling fruit whenever he could.

One night we were woken up by our landlady, who lived next door. She said she knew we didn't watch television but that we had to see the news. We came over, and her family was watching Peter being arrested by Interpol in Lima. He was wanted for three murders in Bolivia and Chile, all young women.

I was angry I hadn't seen it or sensed it, angry I hadn't apprehended him myself. I didn't want that to happen again. I wanted to see justice.

And I wanted to see Mary.

So I would stick around.

Interrupting my thoughts, the sandwich came, with a side of potato salad. The kraut was made with red cabbage, and the corned beef was thick.

I ate the culinary masterpiece slowly. It is easy to eat too fast, especially when you're hungry and food is good—another habitual pitfall I had trained myself to avoid. That was on account of a conversation I had had with the fittest guy I had ever met, a soldier in Peru who was also something of a strongman. He'd said the secret to fitness was chewing every bite of food thirty times.

I didn't always count, but I had learned to savor each meal.

After I finished I set my dishes on the edge of the table for easy retrieval, wiped the table with my napkin, and eased back in my seat.

I must have dozed off watching a silent showing of *Shane* on the television, because the next thing I knew I was peeling my forehead off the table at the sound of the door.

Mary.

She looked even better than she had the night before, more radiant. Her cheeks were extra rosy from the cold, and snowflakes hung in her hair and eyelashes.

She saw me and waved. I waved back. With one finger she signaled me to wait and walked back into the kitchen. A moment later she came back without her hat and coat.

It was getting dark outside, and the dinner rush was coming early. People were apparently trying to beat the snow. Unsuccessfully. It was still falling and looked like it would never stop.

Mary sat down.

"Thank you," I said with a yawn.

"For what?"

"For your compliments and for sitting with me."

"You're welcome. So I guess Agnes talked to you?"

"Only briefly. She said you both had something to talk to me about," I said.

"Yes, and it's important. That's why she is closing early."

Agnes bustled by with laden trays. She was working hard and fast, and when Mary moved to help, she just shook her head.

"Agnes doesn't seem to like the police," I said.

"Not *these* police," Mary said, echoing Agnes's earlier words. "You shouldn't have run, by the way. That was stupid; you could have been arrested, or worse."

"Why doesn't she like them?" I asked.

"That's a long story."

"So I keep hearing."

"I'm sure Agnes will tell you about it later, but what we really wanted was to ask you for is your help. Rock and French said Strawn told them you were a Mormon missionary?"

I nodded.

"Well, Agnes's niece, Amy, is having a hard time. She is a sweetheart but a little . . . troubled. Not in a bad way, but there are a lot of dark clouds hanging over her past. It's understandable. She's not off the edge but flirting with it. Rebellious, remote. You know, all the symptoms. There are no drugs yet or anything like that. But you guys are supposed to be good counselors. I mean, I know you're not like an *actual* counselor, but we were thinking you could preach to her. Give her some advice, like as an independent third party. You're a friendly, attractive guy. Maybe she'll listen to you."

A call to serve.

"Absolutely. I am no expert, but I can talk and listen," I said.

"We're getting worried. She didn't come in for work today and hasn't responded to our calls or texts."

"Does that happen a lot?" I asked.

She shook her head. "Never."

I remembered Strawn's words: *I want you to keep what you know quiet, just until we get a read on the situation.*

A murderer on the loose did not bode well for a missing girl. So, I thought for a second and leaned in, lowering my voice.

"Mary, I think you and I need to go see her right now. I got my car back, but the police haven't caught the guy who stole it. He killed someone right before he knocked me unconscious."

Mary showed no sign of distress other than a narrowing of her eyes and a pursing of her lips.

"Let's go," she said. "Let me get my coat."

I moved to wait by the front door.

Mary appeared, all bundled up, and held up her car keys. "Do you have winter tires and chains?" she asked.

"No."

"Let's take my car; it'll handle better."

Her car was the burned-orange Jeep Wrangler I'd noticed the first time I'd gone to the café. It had all the bells and whistles and looked well-suited for the terrain.

We were in a hurry, but I figured there was time for chivalry, so I moved to the driver's side door to open it. It was locked.

Mary looked at me strangely. "I can get my own door."

"I know," I said.

She hit the unlock button, shrugging and smiling. "As long as you know."

She climbed in, and I trekked around to the passenger side. I sat sideways in the seat with my legs hanging out the door and kicked my boots together like Dorothy in *The Wizard of Oz* to knock the snow off.

There's no place like home.

Mary pushed some buttons and pulled some levers, which started the heater running and the windshield wipers working.

I recognized some of the side streets from my earlier escapade. We drove for a few minutes in silence and passed the motel. I looked at Mary; she was picturesque. Her red hair was long and straight and framed her face like petals on a flower, like fire around a burning, bright ember.

She drove with her left hand, resting her elbow on the window ledge.

I broke the silence. "Not that I'm not flattered or anything, but what made you and Agnes think I'm a good fit to help you?"

She smiled and looked at me out of the corners of her eyes. "I told Agnes I thought you seemed genuine and respectful."

We drove on in silence a little more. I was scanning outside the windows for any potential danger.

"What are the odds your attacker got to her too?" she said quietly, as if whispers lessened the likelihood of evil.

"Nine hundred and sixty to one," I said.

She gave me a funny look.

"The population," I said.

The snow was so heavy the flakes reflected the headlight beams back at us like miniature supernovas. We could have been driving in circles. Or into the middle of the woods. Or right off the edge of the world.

"Odds are getting better," I said. "No way would he have hiked all the way out here, not in this."

Mary nodded, said nothing.

"So why not go to the police?" I asked.

She shifted in her seat, like her heater was getting too hot. "Agnes thinks they're all useless. I don't think they're all that bad."

"And Amy lives alone?" I asked.

"Yes."

"Where are Amy's parents?"

"That's what I meant by dark clouds. Agnes raised her because Amy's mom was viciously attacked when she was pregnant. She lived long enough to deliver Amy, but that was it. There was no sign of her dad, and they never found the killer."

"Could have been one and the same."

She shivered. "It's just awful."

It was, and I was sorry to hear it. I didn't get any more background because, just then, we saw more lights, some white, some red and blue, strobing and washing across the snow and the trees.

Three police vehicles huddled around the smoldering remains of a house, like wolves gathered to a carcass. The officers were spread out and moving around the smoking heap, flashlights blazing.

Mary pulled up short, her whole body going rigid. My blood chilled for a beat, and the ancient part of my brain waved a red flag behind my eyes.

Danger. Fight or flight, the most fundamental binary decision in the world.

"Stay in the car," I said, stepping out into the cold light of night.

Flashlight beams played over me, and I shielded my eyes.

"Sawyer?" Strawn said. "What are you doing here?"

"We were coming to check on Amy," I said.

Rock moved by us, glaring at me and motioning for Mary to get out of the jeep. French was squatting close to the burned ruins, maybe looking for clues, maybe for warmth.

"There's no sign of her," Strawn said.

"Do you think the bad guy got her?"

Strawn swallowed slowly, like his mouth was dry or he was balancing his words, like a smart guy who thought before he spoke. "Did you tell anyone about your accident?"

Collision.

"No."

"Then, what are you doing here?" he asked, stepping forward. His back blocked the headlight beams from his car, silhouetting him against the glare, and his shadow stretched over me.

"I didn't think my problem had anything to do with Amy. Mary just wanted to check on her. She was worried about getting stuck, so she brought me along," I fibbed.

"You seem to be making yourself right at home, Sawyer. Does Miss Mary think you capable of lifting four thousand pounds?"

"Not all at once," I said, remembering too late Washington's nineteenth rule: *Let your countenance be pleasant but in serious matters somewhat grave.*

French came and stood next to Strawn; he had a cell phone out and was cupping his hand over the mouthpiece.

"Doc's on the line," he said.

Strawn waved me away, like he was slapping the air with a backhand. "You have a knack for showing up at the scenes of serious crimes, Sawyer. We'll be in touch if we need you. Until then, goodbye."

He took the phone, and I took the hint. I stomped back to Mary, not out of anger, just in trying to stave off the frostbite. She hadn't gotten out but was talking to Rock through her lowered window.

Strawn called to Rock and asked loudly, "Where the devil is Lang?"

Rock hustled back to his boss and stepped right into my way, like he expected me to move. My pride is not so great that I feel the need to rise to every lame challenge, so I stepped aside, thinking Rock was a problem that wouldn't keep much longer.

I climbed back into the Jeep, bringing enough snowflakes for our very own snowball fight.

Mary was biting her lip and kneading the steering wheel, staring straight ahead.

"What did Rock say?" I asked.

"That she isn't here, but as far as they can tell, the fire was started on purpose. They found gasoline splashed around on the walkway."

"Weird," I said.

"What are we going to tell Agnes?"

"Nothing yet. Is there anywhere else Amy could be? Maybe at a friend's or boyfriend's house?"

Mary shook her head. "She doesn't have a boyfriend that I know of."

She started the intricate process of backing up and turning around. We drove back mostly in silence.

There were plenty of explanations for Amy's disappearance, plenty of probabilities, between best- and worst-case scenarios. I was optimistic. Mary wasn't.

"It's going to be okay," I said.

"She could be in danger."

"True. Or, equally possible, she could be safe and sound somewhere. What else did Rock say?"

"Her car is gone."

"There you go," I said. "I found my car clear on the other side of town, and there is no way the bad guy walked from there to here. What kind of car does she drive?"

"A white Mercury Grand Marquis."

"That wasn't the car I crashed with."

"Would you come over?" Mary asked. "I don't want to talk to Agnes alone."

"You live together?"

"I rent her basement," she said.

"Amy didn't want to live there?"

"She is not very social. And she is rebellious."

"But not very," I said, "or she wouldn't have kept working for her aunt. I think she is going to be okay."

We said nothing the rest of the way, which was fine by me because I had time to think and I wanted Mary to be able to concentrate on the task at hand. The roads were invisible, and more than once I thought we were bound for the ditch. But Mary was a good driver, and the winter wheels did their job.

I eventually recognized some of the turns from my earlier exploration in the stolen police car. We ended up at the end of the nine o'clock spoke, close to the main part of town but far enough removed it felt like we were in the frontier.

The snow-covered, paved road ended at a nondenominational church. A dirt path covered in filthy snow extended a couple hundred yards from there. I couldn't tell what was beyond because of the thick trees.

The Jeep bumped along, passing the church and skirting a metal mailbox as Mary turned down the long drive. Now I could see some lights winking from a distance between the trees. Agnes lived in a prosperous house situated in such a way as to be near enough to neighbors without being too close.

"You sure Agnes won't mind my being here? I mean, I'm not a bad guy, but I wouldn't expect two women out in the middle of nowhere to take a big ugly stranger's word on that."

"You're not ugly," Mary said. "And you're welcome here. You're helping us out."

"I haven't helped at all so far."

"I think you will. You seem like a useful kind of guy to have around."

Nice but inaccurate.

CHAPTER SEVEN

AGNES'S HOUSE WAS NOT THE little country cottage I had antici-pated. It wasn't in the low ranch style I had seen in town either. It was ornate without being opulent. There was a wraparound porch, wide enough for rocking chairs, and there were tons of windows with open green shutters against white fish-scale siding. In front of a heavy door was a worn welcome mat.

The entryway was hardwood that ran straight into the kitchen, where Agnes was moving about. To the right was a sitting room, carpeted with a thick shag. Agnes had a piano, a love seat, and a couch, neatly arranged. Pictures and needlepoints hung on the walls. Maybe she'd inherited them from family members and now displayed them proudly. I saw a woodburning stove and an empty box beside it.

Agnes was opening cupboards and pulling stuff out—teas and other assortments. She must have seen us driving up and gotten right to playing hostess.

"Mr. Sawyer," she said, "would you be so kind as to fetch some wood for the stove?"

I nodded. "Of course, ma'am."

Mary was pulling off her shoes. "Thanks, Sawyer. You'll need a coat. There's one in the closet that might fit. We'll talk in a bit?"

I nodded, found the only coat that was not small and feminine, and let myself out, again wondering who in heaven had set the switch to snow and forgotten about it. But the coat was a luxurious item, leather with furry lining and a big collar.

It looked like an old-fashioned bomber jacket. It fit fairly well, except across the shoulders, and the sleeves were too short.

I wondered whose it was.

Stepping carefully off the porch, I trudged around to the back of the house, where I rightly assumed a shed would be. Pressed up against the side of the shed was an adequate stack of wood. The shed door was pretty rusted or frozen and required a number of pushes and pulls before granting me entry. I found a string to a weak yellow bulb that illuminated the cramped, dusty space, but only just.

The shed was full of things I like, and I like a lot of things. In fact, I am pretty sure most people can find more things they like than things they don't. And I like sheds, mostly because they are full of tools, and tools mean building. And creativity, not cleanliness, is next to godliness.

But being clean can help.

After an appropriate amount of rummaging through scrap lumber, near-empty paint cans, and boxes of nails, I found a double-bit axe. If I had known I would be playing Paul Bunyan, I would have grabbed the pilfered axe out of my car. But the double-bit worked just fine. The wood split easily, and soon I was in a rhythm: set a piece on the block, swing, chop, set again. Though, with each *shunk* of the axe I felt a twinge in my skull. I became aware of small pains from the crash that I hadn't noticed before. Muscles were strained, stiffened, and sore.

But it wasn't the worst I'd had.

I was getting a nice stack by the time I realized I hadn't asked exactly how much Agnes needed. I figured what I had cut would be enough. And if it wasn't, I could always get more, but there was no way of putting together what I had already split. I didn't want to make too much kindling and leave too few bigger chunks. It's like cutting hair—better not to take too much too fast.

I didn't want to deplete her supply that was no doubt calcu-lated to last the whole rest of the winter.

I stopped and listened. My breath fogged before my eyes. While working, I had forgotten the weather. It had my attention now. The searching fingers of cold found me, even with the warm coat. The air tasted sharp, biting the back of my throat with each intake.

It was still snowing.

The silence was heavy. Incredibly so. Not oppressive, just reassuring in a firm, stern way. It felt wrong to break it with any more noise beyond the rhythmic percussion of the axe and the beat of my steps, so I just breathed and listened, churning the many happenings of the past day over in my mind, thinking about how I was going to break the bad news about Amy.

Silence and bad news: two tough things to break.

I imagined Agnes and Mary fixing tea and maybe some cookies, the kind of comforting busy work that staves off impending doom and gloom.

I turned my gaze back to the house; lights were on, and it looked like an island in a sea of snow.

It is easy to get lost in thought. I certainly was.

Until something brought me crashing back to reality.

I am not a believer of mysticism. I do not think people have a sixth sense, third eye, second sight, or whatever. I am sure the stars don't dictate the lives of earthlings.

But I do know that if you train yourself to be aware, really aware, of yourself and your surroundings, then you can pick up on certain things. For example, you can walk into a house and know whether or not it's occupied simply by the absence or presence of almost-imperceptible human vibrations. Or you can go to bed with a problem in mind and wake up with the answer. Or feel eyes on the back of your head. Your primordial brain kicks in, and the hairs up on the nape of your neck stand up.

That's what happened to me right then.

I was facing the rear of the house and could see the warm light reaching out of the many windows. I saw Mary's Jeep in the driveway and the unpaved road wandering off into the trees. I knew the church was behind me, and I've never been afraid of churches. But there was a thick stand of evergreens between me and the place of worship.

I turned in what I hoped was a casual, unhurried manner, like I was just a guy admiring his surroundings, but there was nothing I could make out between the low branches.

I have been all over the world, for one reason or another, in some pretty rough places with some pretty tough customers. But at least, in those places, I had always been face-to-face with my assailants, like that would-be mugger in Peru.

I was sure I was looking right back at whoever was looking at me.

The ancient inclination to fear what I couldn't see, the realization that something was out there, was a feeling I had trained myself to suppress. *Lean forward instead of back. Face the fear. Fight or flight?*

I did neither. Yet.

I had an axe, which was useless at this range. But I reasoned if the guy was staring at me down the barrel of a rifle, he would have taken a shot by now. He might have a handgun, but handguns at that distance would be about as ineffectual as my axe.

I shouldered the axe and took a step forward. *Fight, not flight.*

Honestly I must have looked a little silly, trying to lift my legs above the snow, shuffling like an emperor penguin. But I wanted to make the first move, shake him up a bit. That was one thing I learned from years of hard-won fistfights and boxing matches: if something hurts you, if something scares you, don't back up. Go toward it.

Like in my first-ever boxing match. My opponent busted my nose in the opening round. A broken nose is usually enough to take the starch out of anyone. It hurts, and it makes your eyes water so badly you can't see straight. The nose is an easy target and thus the subject of repeated punishment. But I walked him down and knocked him out.

Sometimes you have to go straight at the danger—go forward, not back.

Which I did. And was brought to the immediate conclusion that I had been wrong in my assessment. A thunderous *crack* split the silent night in half.

I thought I'd been shot.

I fell back in a sitting position, deep into the snow, dropping the axe, and rolled over toward the shed and away from the house. The wood might stop a bullet, but the windows wouldn't. I didn't want to think about Agnes or Mary getting hurt.

I had never been shot at before, actually shot at. I had seen both ends of a gun, very recently, in fact. But they had always gone unfired. I scrambled up, breathless and covered in snow, pressed up against the far side of the shed.

I had few options. Very few. Making a run for the house was not one of them. That would present a unified target of Agnes, Mary, and me. I couldn't stay where I was because all the shooter had to do was stroll up out of the forest and pick me off at his leisure.

So I did something stupid, which ended up being my initial plan all over again, just in fast motion. I yelled and whooped, taking off at a staggering, lumbering run, pumping my knees high, right toward where I thought he'd be. A hundred yards is really a very short distance when you are running, even through heavy snow. But before I was halfway to the trees, I saw the limbs move and heard shuffling and scrambling. There were two people, not one. They were retreating. I kept going, a little slower.

Pushing against the fragrant pines, I was too late to see them. They were gone. They must have had a car waiting.

Then I saw that I had been more wrong than I thought. Or, rather, I *heard* I was wrong. For all my love of trees and all the time I've spent among them on trails in Washington, I had never seen one break from winter weather. The *crack, crash* I had taken to be a gunshot was a branch, overladen with snow, that had snapped off one of the trees in the copse. Nature's powdered sugar was out to get me in more ways than one. If it couldn't freeze me, it would scare me to death.

The noise had been surprising, especially on top of being watched by persons unknown whom I knew had ill-intent. But, upon reflection, there was a stark contrast between the branch snap and the sound of a gunshot. Even among firearms sound varies, but with all, there is a distinctive *smack* or *bang*, and that usually echoes and reverberates more than nature noises. Sometimes people mistake the backfire of an engine or fireworks for a gunshot, but even those are different.

I came back toward the house, kicking myself a little. If I hadn't fallen, I might have caught them. But whoever they were, they seemed uncommitted to action, for now. I was sure they wouldn't try anything again anytime soon.

The lights looked inviting, and a fire sounded good.

After some digging, I found the axe, dried it off on my shirt, and sunk it into a log in the shed to keep its edge. Then, with an armful of wood, I went back to the house.

Mary moved to help me as I balanced the wood in one hand and worked the front door open with the other.

"You must be freezing."

I was, but I wouldn't admit it. "I'm good."

"I saw you from the window. What were you doing at the tree line?"

I saw Agnes arranging the table and didn't want to worry her.

"Later," I said in an undertone.

I stomped snow from my boots and got busy building a fire. I guess that's another thing Boy Scouts had taught me, or at least given me the chance to practice, in addition to just being prepared. But really I attribute any worthwhile life lesson solely to my father. Once the flames caught I closed the slit door to the stove and arranged the rest of the wood.

Agnes invited me to wash up. I found the bathroom down the short hallway, past a few more portraits.

My hands were still a little numb, so I ran cool water over them until the feeling came back. I splashed my face and combed my hair with wet fingers.

I looked in the mirror and sighed. That was about as good as it was going to get; it might or might not have been good enough for Mary, not that romance fit high on my list of priorities at the moment, if I had a list. Which I didn't.

The first thing on it would have been to find my car. Check. Next thing, food. Helping find Amy was paramount. And finding the guy who had whacked me on the head was right there near the top, too, not so much for myself—I can let things go. Usually. *Turn the other cheek and all that. Though it certainly was not my favorite feature of Christianity.*

But I don't like evildoers getting away with doing evil. I hadn't asked to end up in the middle of a murder and possible missing-person case, but here I was. And even though Strawn had pushed me to stay well enough away, I couldn't let Agnes and Mary worry themselves about Amy all alone.

People excuse themselves from helping others with all kinds of flimsy rationalizations—*it's not my business, not my problem, someone else will handle it*—and, of course, the buck keeps getting passed. But I believe anybody's problem is everybody's problem, so it might as well be me who helps out.

There was a knock at the door.

"Sawyer? Are you all right?"

I opened up. Mary was standing there, arms crossed, like she was cold. Or uncomfortable. The self-assurance and supreme confidence had faded. She was sharing the strain and sadness and the worry about Amy.

She still looked great. She had changed into a pair of sweatpants and an oversized shapeless sweater that somehow accentuated her figure. The sleeves went all the way down to her fingertips, and the hem ended halfway between her waist and her knees.

"Sorry. Just thinking," I said.

She gave me a halfhearted smile. "I thought maybe you had fallen in love with your own reflection."

"Not yet. Not ever. I'm no Narcissus."

We walked single-file back to the kitchen. With a certain air of decorum incident to gracious hosts, Agnes motioned for us to be seated.

Agnes served cocoa for me, and she and Mary dabbed their bags of tea in and out of their little ceramic teacups, which were exquisitely decorated in a princess pattern of pastel-colored flowers and swirls. They looked too fancy for me. My finger barely fit through the handle. The cocoa was good though—better even than at the café. That was an upward trend I could get used to:

first Strawn's generic cup, then the Oak Table's, and now Agnes's
home brew.

We didn't say anything for a long while. Just blew steam and
sipped and sat.

I didn't hear any more branches break. I just looked at the
dregs of my cocoa. They didn't tell me anything, like people think
tea leaves tell fortunes.

"We weren't close."

I looked up at Agnes. Waited for more. She continued. "By
the time my sister died, I realized we hadn't spoken in a year
anyway, so nothing much changed, really. Sometimes I think she
is still alive, just not talking to me."

"What happened?" I asked.

"Twenty-five years ago my sister, Arlene, ran away; I was still
in high school. But I think *ran away* is a bit misleading. It was
more like a benign kidnapping. You know how it is when they
think they're in love. She wound up in Washington state. After a
while she became pregnant, and at thirty-eight weeks she was . . .
bludgeoned . . ."

Mary covered her mouth and looked away. I didn't think she
had the stomach for any kind of violence or tragedy, which spoke
of the greatness of her soul.

It is not a good thing to be desensitized to gruesomeness.

"We didn't even know she was expecting. She lived just long
enough for them to save the baby, baby Amy."

"Was the killer Amy's father?" I asked.

"That is what everyone figured. But they never found him.
Arlene never spoke of him before she left; we never got phone calls
or letters. But eventually the police reasoned it was a stranger; there
were plenty of no-accounts rolling through Seattle back then."

Still are, I thought.

"But you thought otherwise?" I asked.

"I *know* otherwise. It *was* Amy's father."

"How do you know?" I asked.

"Well, isn't it always? They never found him. He never surfaced. I brought Amy back here and raised her. When Strawn

became the chief of police, I asked him for help, you know, to keep the case open or something. I thought having an ally on the inside might help. But he never seemed to follow through on it. Nothing ever seemed to happen. Now Amy is running the risk of ending up like her mom. I don't want her to leave Cluff."

"Agnes, I believe families can be together forever. Every family has issues, but over time, things tend to work out. I'll do what I can to help."

Agnes smiled sadly, reaching out to touch my hand. "Keep the fire going, will you? I'm tired. It has been a long day. I'm going to bed."

She started to clear the saucers and cups. I stood up. "Let me."

"There's no dishwasher, I'm afraid."

"No problem. I prefer doing dishes by hand." There is something soothing about washing dishes manually, seeing the immediate fruits of your labors. Something starts dirty and ends up clean.

"I should put you to work in the restaurant."

"I'd do it for free just to eat there." I smiled a little, hoping to cheer her up.

It didn't work. Maybe I had reminded her Amy was an AWOL employee on top of being her flesh and blood. She sighed, tried to smile, and sighed again. She was really trying. Emotions that are only mostly pent-up must be hard to handle, like opening a can of soda pop after shaking it in an industrial-grade paint mixer.

Agnes disappeared down the hallway. I heard a door close and some water run.

Mary joined me at the sink, and together we washed, rinsed, and dried.

"I appreciate you trying to help. I just don't see how to break the news about Amy's house," she said.

"We'll wait until we know more, but we won't wait forever. It wouldn't be right not to tell her." I turned off the faucet.

Mary was handling the stress pretty admirably. She looked a little wan, but keeping Agnes afloat seemed to help ease the crushing weight of worry.

Sense of purpose is good that way.

Stepping away from the sink, she motioned me to follow.

"Let's go downstairs. You can dry your clothes and shower if you want. It'll warm you up. I'm tired, too, but you have to tell me what was happening outside."

"Okay."

I replaced the teacups and saucers on the shelves and added fuel to the stove. I tried to calculate the burn rate and hoped I'd brought in enough.

I moved to the entryway, checked outside the door, and then closed and locked it. I made sure the windows were locked too. Most small towns aren't in the habit of securing households, but given the recent prowling and the lack of results by Cluff's finest, I thought it prudent.

The staircase to the basement was short and the ceiling low. It was cozy, though, if a little colder than the upstairs.

Mary curled up on a leather sofa, with an Indian blanket, and turned on a movie about an orange fish. The television was normal-sized, not like the monstrosities some people spend fortunes on. She pointed behind her to a door. "Bathroom's through there. Help yourself to anything you want. It's all pretty girly though."

"Works for me. Thanks."

The bathroom was pretty girly, but not in a typical pink and bubbly, rainbow-unicorn sort of way. It had just the right amount of feminine charm in the form of fluffy white towels, seashell-shaped soaps, and more mirrors than a carnival funhouse. It was also spacious, with plenty of shelf room. There were all sorts of potions and lotions, coconut-scented concoctions that made miraculous and misleading claims: *Natural-looking hair, Leaves skin feeling hydrated,* and other nonsense.

The shower stall was next to a set of front-loading washing and drying machines. On top of the washing machine I found a less-deceitful detergent. It only promised to clean clothes, which was all it needed to do.

So I set my pocket junk out of the way and made sure my cash and passport weren't wet from my rolling around in the snow. Then

I stripped down and followed the instructions for a "quick wash," which involved a lot of twisting and pulling of knobs. It rattled and hissed and made all kinds of inexplicable noises.

I didn't want to be standing around waiting for the cycle to finish, so I found something useful to do. I still had my toothbrush from the inn. Mary had lots of different flavors of toothpaste. Different sizes, too: small travel-sized tubes and big eight-ounce containers. I picked the one that was fullest since I figured that was her least favorite, or at least the one she could spare the most of, and cleaned my teeth.

I showered with the water as hot as I could stand then brushed my teeth again. I switched my clothes to the dryer, checking the lint catcher per the instructions. It was clean and clear.

I figured I had some time until my clothes were dry, so I delved deeper into the assorted toiletries. I found a pack of disposable razors that weren't pink next to a can of shaving cream labeled for men.

I imagined Mary as some sort of bearded woman, like in a circus. I would have still found her attractive. Probably. More likely the razors and cream were from a recent boyfriend. So I broke open the pack and shook the shaving-cream can vigorously, per instructions, and gave myself a much-needed razoring. I had already lost the mission habit of shaving daily, so I shaved twice, partly because I had missed some spots and partly to stick it to Mary's ex.

It's important to not only beat your enemies but also make sure they know they've lost. The ex might come back one day and ask for his stuff and would find it used, much to his chagrin.

Of course, I'd be long gone by then. Probably.

I let the flannel button-up tumble a little longer, along with my socks. Everything else was pretty much dry, so I put my pants and undershirt on.

When I came out Mary was simultaneously watching the movie and texting.

"Thank you," I said.

"It was as much for me as you. You needed it."

I said nothing.

Mary said, "Sorry. I'm kidding. Just trying to lighten the mood. Sit down."

I sat.

She offered me a corner of the blanket and slid a little closer.

"So, about outside . . . ," she said.

"Whoever it was, they weren't coming to Christmas carol. There were two of them."

"Carter and Rock?"

"Maybe, or maybe worse. It's conceivable Strawn wanted them to make sure I am not meddling anymore, or they could still be sore about earlier."

"You shouldn't have picked on them."

"They were picking on me. Well, Rock was, at least. French isn't bad."

"Just be careful."

"I will," I lied.

"They said you were a missionary in Peru. What was it like?"

"Hot. Beautiful. It was a real culture shock. We get so comfortable in our First World, and we forget we're all the same people in the same basic condition, with the same needs. We magnify what little differences there are and set aside our two most important imperatives."

"Which are?" she asked.

"To love God and our neighbor."

"To love and be loved," she said. "Sounds nice. Do you love people?"

"More than anything. In Peru I met people who mattered so much in the moment, and then the moment changed, and it was on to the next. I would like nothing more than to see the faces of every person I served, but I'll probably never see them again."

"Until heaven?"

I smiled. "You got that right."

She took my right hand, inspecting it as closely as a palm reader.

"That's the first thing I noticed about you. Your hands. They are soft and gentle but clearly hardworking."

I grinned. "Most people comment on my eyes or smile, if anything."

"They're nice too."

"What did you tell me yesterday about flattery?"

She let go of my hand.

"It's not flattery if it's true." She smiled.

"Thanks."

We sat and watched the movie. Mary sent the occasional text message. She said she was reaching out to mutual acquaintances of Amy's, seeing if anyone knew her whereabouts.

My stomach started to growl just as the movie hit a suspenseful juncture.

"You hungry?"

"Starving." Which was hyperbole, of course.

We went upstairs, and while I stoked the fire, she made cold-cut sandwiches with spicy mustard and some greenery I took to be kale. Sometimes there's no telling with vegetables.

Or people, for that matter; they'll always surprise you.

We cleaned up quietly, and I went around checking the windows again.

It was snowing outside, but nothing was stirring like on the night before Christmas—not even a mouse, as far as I could tell.

On tiptoe we went back downstairs. The movie looked to be wrapping up nicely. Every fish seemed happy.

We were semiconsciously avoiding the serious stuff, which I was fine with because, like I had told the cops, Mary was the first girl I had talked to with any hint of romantic intentions. Mary was a very pretty and pleasant girl. She had looked good when we first met. She looked great up close.

I thought of something to talk about.

"Does it always snow this much in winter?"

She smiled, with a little air of superiority. "You want to talk about the weather? Isn't that a little mundane and cliché?"

"On the contrary," I said. "Nothing could be more pertinent. I mean, think about it: the weather impacts our lives more directly than most other things."

She gave me a funny look. "You mean, like seasonal affective disorder?"

"What?" I asked.

"It's a kind of depression because of the changes in the seasons."

"That's a weird thing to get depressed about," I said, which was insensitive of me.

"It's pretty common, actually. And as an acronym it spells SAD, which is interesting."

I nodded. "I meant the weather brought us together. If it hadn't been for the snow and the crash, we would never have met."

She shook her head. "No, we met because we decided to talk to one another."

She was right, of course.

She continued. "Okay, now that we're done with the boring weather report, let's go on to entertainment. What kind of music do you like?"

That is a common question, and all the time you hear vague answers: *I like a little of everything, depends on my mood, anything but country.* Which is all well and good, but specificity is helpful and demonstrates a degree of thought and consideration to inquiries like that. I pursed my lips, thinking. I don't have a HiFi system or a CD collection or an mp3 player or whatever people buy nowadays. But I like music.

"I like guys like Jim Croce and Gordon Lightfoot. Of course, I'm a bit of a sucker for Adele and Dido."

"I've never heard of Jim Crowfoot or Jordan whatever."

I laughed. I thought it would be polite to ask her taste in diversion, and besides that, I actually wanted to know, but she had a far-off look in her eyes. Maybe she was just tired.

We sat there in comfortable silence.

I am no kind of mind reader—I don't believe in that stuff—but I could see the wheels turning under her red hair. She was working around to the nitty-gritty. She looked at me pointedly, and I thought she was going to ask more questions. She didn't.

"I wish you wouldn't mess with Carter and Rock. You stole their car."

SUV, and they left it running.

I sighed. I don't like to argue. I am a peace-loving man. "Strawn didn't seem to mind. They were gunning for me, so it seemed the best solution."

Mary settled back against the arm of the couch, farther away from me. Not a good sign.

Her eyes drifted back to the movie; the credits were rolling. "We used to date, you know."

"You and Strawn?"

She pulled an incredulous grimace. "No, gross. Me and Rock."

"He is pretty handsome." I had to say something.

"I guess I equated good-looking-ness with goodness. My mistake."

"It happens to the best of us and the rest of us." I patted her foot. "And you're the best of us, Mary."

"You barely know me."

"I guess I must be coming to the same conclusion about good-looking-ness and goodness."

She laughed, a little self-deprecatingly.

I thought more about what she had said about being duped by Rock. I wanted to ask what had happened, but I thought it might be too personal.

I couldn't remember if there was a George Washington rule about such things. Probably. *Ungentlemanly to inquire.*

Moving so I was back against the opposite arm of the couch, I looked at her. "You can never be too sure about people; they'll always surprise you, sometimes for good, sometimes for bad, but either way, at least you know."

She pondered that. "So 'don't judge a book by its cover' sort of thing."

Again I wanted to ask what was so bad about Rock, mostly out of concern for Mary, partly to vindicate my own dislike of him. But I didn't.

"Carter's not bad, like you said," she continued. "He got teased a lot in school for being chubby. So did I, come to think of it."

"I think you're beautiful, Mary. Inside and out, and I think French will make a good cop." I didn't care about Carter French.

Plenty of people get made fun of. I know I did. It's no excuse for turning out mean. But I didn't say that. Mary seemed a lot nicer than me.

Mary stretched her feet out, ignoring my compliment. I kept my legs bent; I would have been putting my toes in her face otherwise, which is inadvisable on a first date. Or any date. If this was a date at all.

"Did you grow up here?" I asked.

"Born and raised. My dad lives in Troy. He runs a small motor-repair shop. My mom died when I was sixteen."

Too much sadness for such a small town.

"I'm sorry to hear that."

"Not your fault." She smiled a little mischievously as she repeated my response to her sympathy from the night before.

She closed her eyes, resting her head on the armrest. Didn't say anything more.

Both Mary and Agnes were awfully trusting of a big strange man who had just happened to wind up in town. I wasn't complaining. And I wasn't a threat. But plenty of guys are. I would have to explain to them that they shouldn't make a habit out of housing transients.

I had a lot more questions than answers at that point and absolutely no idea where to begin. But I figured I could give myself a break, just long enough for some shut-eye. It wasn't a very big couch, but it was plenty comfortable, and I can fall asleep anywhere. I stifled a yawn.

I groped around on the floor for the remote control. Most power buttons are on the upper left-hand corner. This one was. I turned the screen off and listened in the dark.

Listened to the night sounds of an old cozy house, listened to Mary's slow and steady breathing. I thought of the innkeeper, getting paid for nothing.

I closed my eyes gratefully and gave one last listen for good measure.

And heard a car's engine.

My car's engine.

CHAPTER EIGHT

I AM NO KIND OF gearhead. I don't know much about cars. Just the basics. But that big V8 was unmistakable.

I grabbed at my pocket. There was the key. The *spare* key.

My Buick, taken from the restaurant parking lot, was being driven by parties unknown right outside. I slid out from under the blanket, slowly. Controlled. I did not want to wake Mary. And what was I going to do? Run after them barefoot in the snow?

No, fretting uncontrollably would do me no good. Besides, where could they go? Not out of town.

But the real questions were how had they found me? Were the watchers in the woods the ones in my car now? And if so, why had the driver first shown up on foot? And who was his partner?

I imagined Rock and French in a clandestine meeting with the murderer, adding me to the hit list. But that seemed unlikely. I didn't think they were killers. Just two country boys who never really grew up, stuck in Nowheresville all their lives.

The real killer still had my car key. But how had he tracked me here? Maybe he hadn't. Maybe this was a belated revenge against all of Agnes's family. He had killed Arlene way back when and then maybe Amy just recently. Now he was coming for Agnes. He might not even know I was still here.

Again I thought back to the tree-line incident. There had definitely been two then, but I was sure no one else had been with the killer when we'd crashed. So someone was helping him. And who had the FBI guy been?

I fetched my flannel shirt and socks from the dryer as quietly as I could. I left the dryer door open because it would have made a sharp sound otherwise. The little light in it burned softly. I took one last look at Mary, and then I padded upstairs and slid my boots on. Looking out the window, I didn't see headlights. Obviously. This was a nefarious nighttime ride for the car thief. The car stood out plainly, though, against the snow. It looked hulking and sinister in the dark, like a giant wolf stalking prey.

The thief had driven farther down the dirt road and turned around—for a quick getaway, no doubt.

I was lacing up my boots, wishing I knew where Agnes kept her varmint gun. Surely she had one. It's almost compulsory in Montana. I went to the closet and checked the corners for a shotgun—nothing—and then grabbed the loaned coat.

I heard the car door open. The engine was still running. This was it. He was coming to the house, maybe to break in and shoot Agnes, maybe to torch the whole place. I considered waiting until he tried the door and surprising him, just like he had me, but I decided against that. If he meant to burn the house, I didn't know where he would start. I couldn't put out the fire and fight him at once, especially if he had a partner with him, so I settled on immediate action. It is usually the best approach.

I unlocked the door and charged. There was no way for me to engage the deadbolt without a key, so all I could do was close it.

There was the car, at the end of the drive, by the mailbox. The driver was startled when he saw me but recovered quickly, bolting back the way he had come. Clearing the steps in a single bound, I ran for the car, slipped, and kept going, picking each step up high to clear the snow. He was shorter than me, but he had a head start. Expertly, he stepped in his own footprints he had left in his initial approach.

I broke off from his trail to try and cut the distance and head him off before he could get away, slipped again, recovered, and picked up the pace. I was going to catch him. I thought. He slid across the hood and back into the car just as I grabbed the passenger handle. Locked.

He drove. I held on and ran, my feet slipping on the snow and ice. He sped up.

If this had been a movie, I could have punched through the glass and climbed through, but it wasn't, and I couldn't. He turned sharply by the church, and I lost my grip. I felt my left elbow crater my own quarter panel as I slipped and fell. I tumbled and rolled and narrowly avoided being run over.

Painful, and expensive for me later on, whenever I got my car back. Again. If I got it back. Of course, that was pretty low on the priority list right then.

I lay in the snow, freezing. It was still snowing. I blinked and blew flakes from my nose and eyelashes. I breathed hoarsely. I stood up slowly; I had gotten scraped and dirty from the fall. So much for having just showered and done laundry.

I considered going back, but I was closer now than ever to solving this, and I didn't want to give up so soon. I was responsible for the crash, which initially I had felt bad about but not anymore. I had stopped the escape of a dangerous fugitive. But I wondered why he hadn't finished me off at the crash site. Maybe he had been too spooked or too weak from the ordeal. Maybe he'd just wanted to get away. I was supremely confident in my ability to handle him face to face. In all my fights, I have never been knocked out—not even knocked down— so it was a blow to my ego that he had managed to render me unconscious.

I brushed the snow off as well as I could. If I had thought it was cold during the day, I didn't know the word for it now, in the middle of the night. I heard my breath crackling, felt my cheeks freezing. I set off in what I thought was the approximate direction the thief had taken. I jogged a little, a shuffling, loping stride to keep from slipping and to conserve energy. I shadowboxed, too, throwing punch combinations, bobbing, and weaving, all to keep warm. The trick is to not be too active in the cold. If you move too fast and too hard, you'll sweat. And when you eventually stop, all that sweat will freeze, and you'll be worse off than if you had never moved at all.

All the houses I passed were dark. I might have gone back to Agnes's and called the police, but this was my mission, and the police were questionable at best. Stubborn and foolish as it may seem, I figured I knew what I was doing. I had survived this long, right?

My breath steamed in front of me, and each intake burned the back of my throat. If I had to stay out all night, I would probably die; it was that cold. The snow kept falling, like silent, incessant airstrikes.

I saw no sign of my quarry. I began to get closer to the heart of town and kept going, looking for the freshest ruts in the snow. I was panting doggedly.

The roads were familiar but didn't look quite the same as before. Maybe because I was on foot this time.

I continued on until I got back to where I had started yesterday: the police station, center of town, like a spider's web. It was lit up bright. There was some kind of operation going on. A van was parked outside, and I saw two people going back and forth from the building, carrying large items.

I looked again to be sure I was seeing the right place, but I had no idea what I was looking at. Standing still wasn't doing me any good. My teeth were chattering like a jackhammer. So I continued forward with an almost-audible groan from my frozen joints, like the creaking of a wooden ship lost in the North Pole.

Obviously the operation couldn't be any sort of criminal activity. The people carrying the stuff were right out there in the open, plain as day, except, of course, that it was the middle of the night.

Drawing nearer, I could make out writing on the side of the van. *Cobalt Cleaning.*

The two people looked to be a married Hispanic couple. They were middle-aged and looked cheerful enough about the work.

"Good evening," I said in Spanish. Chivalrous is an easy thing to be when all you have to do is carry stuff, so I offered to help. With a little bit of surprise, the woman consented. I hefted a big vacuum-looking thing. It wasn't heavy for me but probably would have been for her. I was worried I would drop it, though, on account of my feelingless fingers. But I made it inside okay. It was warm, even though the fire was long-extinguished. The station probably had a central heating unit and the fire was mostly for show.

The husband grabbed the last boxes of cleaning supplies—shampoo, maybe. I don't know much about building maintenance. I do know I sure missed American edifice floor covering while I was a missionary. Every floor I saw in Peru was either tile, cement, or dirt.

"Thank you," the man said as I set down the thing. He seemed just as eager to practice his second language as I was to practice mine.

I nodded and smiled. They set about cleaning, paying me no more mind. I was where I probably shouldn't have been, but they didn't know that, which was fine with me. I needed to thaw anyway. I was close to the coldest I had ever been.

I went through the door Strawn had first emerged from when we had met and found myself back among the police desks, not really knowing what I expected to find. Counting Lang's station out front, there were only three occupied workspaces. French's was pretty obvious, with candy wrappers and an unwashed mug. Rock's screen saver was a picture of Mary and him. I bumped the mouse with my knuckle to make it go away, and a blue screen appeared in its place, asking me for a password. I tried typing *Mary.*

Password incorrect.

It was worth a shot.

I was not worried about fingerprints at that point. If my prior offenses weren't enough to land me in jail, then a little computer hacking was not likely to be enough to tip the scales against me.

There was an unopened bottle of mineral water that I helped myself to. Breaking the seal, I drank the whole thing at once and replaced it, empty, onto his desk. When it is cold outside, you don't realize how thirsty you can get.

On top of a pencil sharpener was an unframed photograph of Mary, a studio shot, professional, not just from a disposable camera. I turned it over to see if there was anything written. It said, *Love, Mary*, in blue ink. She had very nice penmanship. *Pen*woman*ship?*

Pocketing the picture, I looked around for any unclaimed edibles.

I was hungry as well as thirsty.

I went back to French's desk. Nothing to eat there that was untouched. There was no personalized screen saver. I tried typing *password* for the password. It was worth a shot.

Password incorrect.

I typed *French*. Nothing doing.

Some people are pros at deciphering passwords and cracking codes. I am not one of them. You ask me to kick down a door or beat some thug up, no problem, but for anything technical I'd be the last pick.

Strawn's office was locked, which was to be expected. Maybe the cleaning crew had a key, but I did not want to ask. I was pushing my luck as it was.

If this had been back before the digital age, I might have been able to open up some old files, cold cases, maybe some clue about Amy, if she had any kind of record.

But computers have advantages, too, because they can access a lot more information than what you can fit into a filing cabinet. I needed some deep background. I needed to know if this was in any way connected to Amy and her mom, needed to know more about the circumstances surrounding Arlene's demise, awful as it surely was, if I was going to be able to prevent further death and destruction.

But I didn't have a password.

French had told Strawn earlier that Doc was on the phone. Strawn had said the doctor pulled double-duty as medical examiner for the police department. *The* doctor, not *a* doctor. There was just one in town, maybe an old guy who still made house calls but without the leeches. I figured he would be a good first point of contact.

I looked around for a phone book, the most unused book ever produced. They show up all the time in people's mailboxes only to collect dust in a cupboard or drawer or on top of the fridge. This is the digital age—no need for print. I found a phone book on a shelf next to *Grey's Anatomy* and *Webster's Dictionary*—maybe they were for the cops to look up words for their report writing—but neither of the volumes looked to have ever been opened. Their spines were seamless.

I flipped through the phone book, looking for anything doctor-related, and found a couple of listings. One was a DDS, a doctor of dental surgery. His name was Pocock. He wasn't the guy I was looking for. My teeth were fine. I brushed three times a day, usually. The second was an E. Pike, MD, for *Medicinae Doctor*. I was a little dismayed to see no mental health specialists. What about all the people suffering from seasonal affective disorder?

I tore the page out of the book. I didn't think it would be missed.

Returning to French's desk, I began looking for something useful. I didn't want to disturb too much. Rock might miss his picture, but he would figure it had slipped between a crevice or something. Probably.

I sat down in French's well-worn desk chair, picking my feet up and giving it a little spin before pulling up like I was ready to work. There was a long thin drawer running the length of the desk right above my legs and three bigger drawers on the right-hand side.

I opened the long one. There were a pad and pen and some sticky notes, gum wrappers, and salt packets. Next I tried the top of the three bigger drawers. There was a stack of old business cards with the Cluff PD logo and the number for Officer Carter French, and there were packaged treats and bags of chips. More office supplies in the next drawer. The bottom drawer was the biggest. We often expect the biggest and the last to be the best. But it wasn't. There were a box of tissues, envelopes, a six-pack of soda pop, and little plastic baggies, maybe for the most miniscule pieces of evidence, like strands of hair or something.

I kept digging. Most people not technology-inclined have a bit more trouble with it, and French did not strike me as a particularly gifted individual. And government computer systems often require frequent password updates. Maybe French had to write his down. But he wasn't careless enough to leave it lying around.

That is when I got creative—creativity is next to godliness, after all—or rather, I reverted to my youth, where the best creativity comes from. Maybe it is the childlike innocence that makes it so.

I rifled through Rock's stuff until I found a pencil and ran it through the electric sharpener Mary's photo had rested on. It buzzed loudly and made me jump a little. Then I took the pencil and pulled the sticky notepad from French's drawer. Like a kid, I rubbed the pencil lightly at a shallow angle all along the top of the pad. When you write on a stack of papers, the pressure from the pen will often indent the underlying page or pages. And if you rub a crayon or a pencil across the indents, like kids do with coins, the shapes will show up.

It worked, which surprised me a little. I felt just like James Bond, except I didn't need a Q. And I lacked the suaveness and the women and the fancy gadgets and the gun. But besides that, I felt pretty cool.

I typed in *@mYs4098.*

It loaded. I was in.

@mY.

Amy.

Interesting.

The numbers and the symbol suggested French had tweaked and changed a similar password slightly each update cycle. I wondered what interest he had in Amy, if it was the same Amy, or if the password even stood for Amy. But I don't like coincidences.

I tore off the page with the password and put it in my pocket. *Leave no trace.*

The screen faded then came back, this time blue with various windows. I didn't really know what I had accomplished. I did not know how to run any of the programs besides the word processor. There was an Internet browser, though, so I double-clicked with the mouse and a new window popped up.

I searched for *Arlene Kirk*. A number of different things popped up. There was a movie star with the same name, and a musician. The browser even made suggestions like *Did you mean James Tiberius Kirk?* as if I didn't know what I wanted.

Maybe most people on the Internet need the extra help. I wouldn't know. I try to avoid computer use as much as possible, hence my incompetence. If I had known how to open the police files on the computer, it would have been easier. So I narrowed the search by adding *Seattle* and *murder* to the search bar.

A number of different links showed up. I clicked the top, which sounded the most relevant. It was old news—very old, from before Google had been created—so I didn't expect a lot. It probably hadn't merited national attention, which was too bad because maybe with more publicity it could have been solved.

I guess there are just too many murders to keep up with. Many wind up unsolved.

The link looked to be a digitized copy of a sidebar written in the *Seattle Times* back in the day. There used to be a time when a newspaper was the lifeblood of any city. Now hardly anyone subscribes to it. They get real-time updates on their phones and tablets instead. All newspaper is good for anymore is wrapping fish, lining kennels, or kindling fires.

The article was short and pragmatic. It said Arlene Kirk had been found on the side of the road in a ditch by a passing trucker. She had been incoherent and bloodied and very pregnant. An ambulance had brought her to the hospital, where the baby was saved but Arlene was not. There had been no clues, no suspects. Police determined she had been attacked somewhere else and driven away from the scene and dumped into the ditch. The article did not reference family members, lifetime achievements, or anything else about Arlene as a person.

There was reference to the potential but unsubstantiated kidnapping from Montana, and the FBI was listed as having no leads.

They had used dogs to sniff out the area. I like dogs a lot. If I ever have a house of my own, I figure I'll have two or three.

I read in a science magazine in a waiting room somewhere that studies show dogs to have developed compassion from centuries of interaction with humans. I believe it is the other way around.

But the police dogs had found nothing. No scent, no sign, no trail. County sheriffs and the state patrol had quickly and quietly filed the event away with the countless other cold cases. The Green River killer was active at that time and mentioned. No solid suspects were listed, though the article hinted at a number of drifters of "dubious character" in the area, which seemed accurate for the greater Seattle area.

The article did not include any photographs or any detail beyond that. I still had so many questions. Where was Amy? Was her disappearance a coincidence? What had the FBI guy been doing with the killer, and why had the agent not advised the Cluff Police of his presence if he had been there in any sort of official capacity? Federal and local law enforcement tended to work in tandem.

The door that led to the lobby opened, and I looked up from a police officer's computer screen, surprised.

It was just the Cobalt crew, the husband and wife, coming to clean the bullpen. I smiled and waved casually, like I was supposed to be there. They went about their work. I was done with mine.

CHAPTER NINE

THE CLOCK IN THE BOTTOM right-hand corner of the screen said it was half past three in the morning.

I was tired and would have to wait for daylight before gathering any more intel. The adrenaline had worn off, and I rubbed my eyes.

I had dated a girl once whose mom had been a sleep doctor. There was a technical name, but I never learned what it was. She told me you shouldn't look at an electronic screen within two hours of bedtime. Something about the blue-green or green-blue light stimulates the brain. It didn't seem to be waking me up at all. I could have folded my arms on the desk and snoozed right then, but I didn't.

Because I remembered Strawn asking where Lang had been when they were at the scene of the house fire. I suddenly worried that the killer and his comrade were perhaps picking off their opposition one at a time. Without a police force, the snowed-in town would be a sitting duck in a frozen pond.

I looked in vain for a way to return the computer to its locked screen. Finding nothing, I just hit a button on the bottom of the monitor that made the screen go dark. Then I went back to the trusty phone book. I found Sergeant Lang easily enough. Tore out the page. I figured I might as well pay him a wellness check. I also looked for Strawn's address, just in case he was in trouble, too, but he wasn't listed. Off the grid. My kind of guy.

Or maybe he had no landline. Just a cell.

I grabbed French's address, too, in case I needed to make a house call there.

I didn't care about Rock.

I looked around one more time, finding nothing of interest. The trip had been fruitful, even if I hadn't caught the killer. I knew a little more than I did before. I had a sense of direction, a starting point in the way of some addresses of people to visit—even though Strawn had told me to stay out, I was counting on him to take all the help he could get as time went on—plus a bottle of water and a photo of a pretty girl. Not bad for a night's work.

I nodded at the cleaning couple and tried to avoid all the wet spots on the floor. I didn't want to ruin their work, which seemed to have been a lot more labor-intensive than mine had been.

When jumping into cold water, the best way was to plunge in, not to wade or tiptoe. So I did that same thing with the frigid night. I started jogging even before the door closed. I thought I heard my car far away. Somewhere a dog barked, and the wind howled. I picked up the pace, painfully. Each breath was laced with daggers of frozen flame. It burned to breathe, and my feet were leaden. I almost tripped once or twice, but I was worried about Mary and Agnes, so I kept a fast pace.

I didn't know when day would break, but in winter the pale-gray light of dawn was often late and only began to show slowly, tentatively, as if of a guilty conscience.

I ran, lengthening my stride as well as I could. I wasn't worried about sweating now. I could stand to freeze a little more.

But that didn't keep my hands from shaking. It was colder than before. To move was all I could think to do—jogging, shadow-boxing, anything to stop my blood from turning to ice and my limbs from snapping off like those branches had at Agnes's.

I could see pretty easily with the reflected and refracted street-lights as I moved along the roads. Then they went out, and it felt ten degrees colder, the silence more oppressive. Power outages had been called for in the news. Here they were. It was not pitch dark though. The white snow seemed to glow ghostily, like it had trapped some of the light or was taking its cue from the shrouded moon. I could see some houses in the distance that still had light, so it wasn't a total blackout.

I've always had a pretty good sense of direction, and Cluff's geography was more straightforward than in most places; it hadn't come without practice though. I'd learned that looking back and memorizing the path behind was a good way to keep from getting lost because things always look different, depending on your direction.

I considered cutting through backyards and fields but concluded that it might take longer, what with all the fence-climbing that way would entail. Besides, some of those homeowners might have mistaken me for a wolf or a burglar or a cattle rustler or whatever and shot me with their compulsory varmint rifles.

If anyone was going to shoot at me, I wanted it to be the criminals because as long as they were shooting at me, they wouldn't be shooting at someone else.

I breathed. Twice in, twice out. I tried to concentrate the oxygen in my mouth, tried to preheat it before it reached my lungs. It didn't work.

I kept running. I realized, with a hint of chagrin, I was violating George Washington's fifty-third rule, to not run in the street, shake the arms, or go up on one's toes in a dancing manner. But I'm not a stickler for rules, no matter how much I admire Washington.

I was getting closer. I could see the church steeple. It had a little white cross at the top.

Sanctuary.

Looking down at my feet, I checked for fresh tracks in the slush. If anyone had driven here in the last little while, it would show. There was nothing new, so I slowed down a bit, stumbling. A nerve near my right shoulder blade felt pinched from the coat. The tightness across the shoulders made me hunch slightly. There was a time when all I would wear was tight shirts to accentuate my muscles. It had been vanity, plain and simple. Once I'd gotten a clue, I'd traded fashion for function. Tight clothes were useless. They limited mobility and left me with less material to fashion a tourniquet or scarf or bag or whatever else you might need in an emergency situation.

I slogged through the snow, passed the mailbox, and collapsed on the porch. I couldn't feel the cold anymore. Or my face, fingers, or toes. On all fours I crawled to the door, steaming like a pile of compost, which is pretty much how I felt. Physically, that is. In every other sense I felt nothing but relief. There was no sign of a forced entry. Agnes and Mary were safe.

I lay on the porch with my feet across the steps, my chest heaving. I rolled slowly over, reaching a hand up to the door, pulling myself up by the knob. It was still unlocked from my hurried departure. Inside, the house was just like I had left it, except the embers in the fireplace had gone out.

My fingers were cold and didn't seem to want to work right. With extra effort I managed to pry my boots off. I didn't think I was anywhere near hypothermic, but I was certainly colder than I wanted to be. I was also more tired than I wanted to be. And hungrier.

However, some things are more important. Like ladies' comfort. So I rekindled the fire, breaking a couple of matches in my fingers, clumsy with cold, before getting it going. I still had no idea what time it was; Agnes's stove did not have a digital component. All I knew was that it was still plenty dark.

Then it was all about not tripping down the stairs. I gripped the handrail so tightly I felt the wall mounts give a little. It wasn't so much that I was worried about hurting myself as I was about waking Mary, not that she needed beauty sleep. She was already beautiful. But sad news and stretched emotions are taxing.

In the dark I made out her shape curled back on the couch. Her cell phone was blinking like she had a message.

I padded quietly into the bathroom, ran my hands under the faucet, and splashed my face. My clothes were once again dirty from rolling around on the road and sweaty from running. So, for the second time in only a handful of hours, I set them to wash. The borrowed coat's tag said, *Dry-clean only,* but I figured that was just a suggestion. Some instructions I follow, some I don't.

I set my pocket junk on the dryer. Everything was intact. I tossed the paper with French's password on it. I didn't want to get all weighed down with luggage.

Then I measured out the detergent and set the knobs the same way as before. The machine started, with all the same sounds, the slow rumble growing steadily into a swishing cadence.

I certainly needed to sleep. I felt like I was a fraying bow being jerked across new strings on a violin. My head ached, not from the car-collision injuries but from a lack of sleep and sustenance.

But I had to shower first. Cleanliness was important, after all, albeit not most.

I started the shower off cool. You never want to get into a hot shower or run your hands under hot water when you're numb. I held my mouth open under the cascade and drank. The water had a metallic hint, nothing I was worried about. Every single tap in the United States is better than what you'll find in Peru.

As feeling flooded back to me, I turned the water steadily warmer until steam filled the bathroom. I took the liberty of using some cleaning agents from Mary's ample supply, notwithstanding their outlandish claims to replenish and beautify. I scrubbed, lathered, and rinsed.

I didn't repeat. Some instructions I choose to ignore.

Afterward I switched my clothes to the dryer and my pocket supplies to the top of the washer, to keep them from rattling. The dryer ran with a bit of racket and a lot of low, rolling hums. I hoped it would just contribute to the ambient white noise and wouldn't wake Mary or Agnes. While I waited I brushed my teeth.

There wasn't much good I could do without at least a couple of hours of shut-eye. Once my clothes were warm and dry, I put them back on, except the jacket. Leaving my flannel button-up untucked, I lay down right on the floor by the couch. I was a missionary. I can sleep anywhere. I had slept in hammocks, on concrete, and in sand-flea-infested quarters in Peru, so the floor was no problem. Positioning my arms under my head, I inhaled and exhaled and was out in seconds.

It could have been seconds, minutes, hours, or years later when I awoke. It wasn't to an alarm clock. That is a habitual pitfall I try to avoid—the ritual of an optimistic setting of the time to awake and then the inevitable bargaining against myself with a tap of the snooze button.

I believe that to awake is to arise—to be instantly alert and ready for action, not to do the groggy, stumbling, half-shut eyes routine. It was more like the flipping of a switch than the rising of the sun. On that particular day I woke up to the smells and sounds of breakfast.

Perfect.

Nothing was better than breakfast. It almost made me forget the danger and bad luck and trouble looming overhead. Bacon crackled and popped in a skillet, and I smelled coffee burbling in a percolator. Mary had evidently covered me in a blanket sometime during the morning. Standing up to tuck in my shirt, I kept smelling and listening and savoring. A whisk was skimming the sides of a glass bowl, maybe making batter for pancakes. I hoped.

Mary and Agnes walked back and forth, talking. I heard their footsteps overhead and their muffled voices.

I brushed my teeth again, without toothpaste, since I planned on eating in the next few minutes. Wetting my fingers under the faucet, I combed my hair as well as I could. Which wasn't very.

That's as good as it's going to get.

Hustling upstairs, I found the kitchen a scene of breakfast nirvana. You would never have known Agnes was in the middle of heartache over a wayward youth coupled with the memories of a departed sister. She was in her element, breaking eggs one-handed over a skillet, flipping bacon and pancakes. Mary set the table deftly. I'm not great at math, but I can count, and there were five places.

We were expecting company.

I offered to help, more than once, but was repeatedly brushed off by flour-dusted hands.

I wanted to ask who else was coming but hesitated for fear of interrupting artists at their work.

"Thank you for letting me sleep in," I said to Mary as she finished filling glasses with water.

"What were you doing on the floor?"

"Sleeping," I said.

She half-smiled, half-frowned. The result was pretty spectacular. She had no makeup on, which complimented her natural beauty. Her long red hair had been brushed into two long curtains down either side of her face, almost reaching her middle. "No, I mean, why were you sleeping on the floor?"

"I went out and didn't want to wake you when I came back."

"I know you went out; I woke up in the middle of the night. Where did you go?"

"I'll tell you later," I said, looking sideways at Agnes, who was plating pancakes and sticking them in the oven to keep them warm.

"Tell me now, Sawyer. I was worried," she said, evenly but with emphasis.

Some instructions I choose to ignore.

"Who's coming to breakfast? I mean, I know I can eat a lot, but this would be a little too much."

It was not a very tactful evasion, but she didn't argue.

"A lonely neighbor and the cook from the restaurant—he can't work whenever we close, so Agnes has him over as a kind of reimbursement for lost wages."

I nodded and said nothing.

I like people. A lot. I can usually find admirable or redeeming qualities in most everyone I meet. Rock excluded. But, given the choice, I'll take my own company. I was disinclined to discuss contemporary events or whatever else breakfast clubs talked about. Especially with the expediency of the work ahead of me. They had asked for my help, and I meant to give it.

Mary was watching me closely, waiting for me to spill the beans about where I'd been, but I said nothing. For now. Timeliness and truthfulness need to coincide in some cases. And I didn't know how

Mary would react to news of my subterfuge until I had something to show for it.

Contrary to popular belief, secrets are no fun to keep. I had to get out of there. As hungry as I was for food, I hungered for justice just as much.

Matthew 5:6 came to mind.

"I need to borrow your car," I said to Mary.

"What about breakfast?" She spoke slowly, her eyes narrowed in concern.

"Save me some, please."

"What are you going to do?"

"Fight some crime."

"That's not your job or your place."

I didn't have time to debate, but I wanted her to understand, if only a little, how I felt.

"Mary, think of every bad thing that has ever happened— every theft, rape, kidnapping, or murder you've ever seen on the news or read about in the paper. Every single one of those horrors could have been prevented if someone had done something differently. You've heard the saying *what goes around comes around.* Well, it's coming around now. The buck stops here. I'm not passing anything else down the row. If I can do something, I should do something. So, are you going to help me or not?"

She didn't look happy about it, but she fished the keys out of the pocket of her coat that was hanging in the entry. "Just be careful."

"You don't have to worry about me."

"I mean with my Jeep; I practically had to sell my soul for that thing."

My track record was not unimpeachable in terms of vehicular care, but I smiled and nodded convincingly, giving her a thumbs-up.

"My apologies to Agnes."

I ran downstairs, grabbed the borrowed coat out of the dryer, and pulled it on. I figured I would need it.

I waited until I got into the Jeep before lacing up my boots.

I did all the things you do when you get into the driver's seat of an unfamiliar car: buzzed back the seat, adjusted the mirrors, and inventoried the dials and knobs. The Jeep was a pretty neat vehicle. I could see how it must have cost a fair bit. I hoped I wouldn't ruin it for Mary, but some things are just beyond your control.

I had to wait a bit for the windshield to fully defrost even after brushing and scraping off snow and ice with a handy tool I found under the backseat.

I drove with a degree of difficulty across the snow-covered road. The snow must have stopped sometime during the night. The sky was still rock solid though. There was no movement, no break in the clouds—just an endless expanse of slate. An ocean of concrete.

I imagined airplanes above the cloud layer, like a vision in a dream, basking in the sun, oblivious to the plight of the earth and its snowbound creatures below.

I like flying. A lot. It never gets old. I took a plane dozens of times in Peru. It was the only way to get out of the rainforest besides the slow crawl of riverboats. It's one of those miraculous things that is scientifically explainable but never really believable, a phenomenon almost as incredible as moms lifting cars off their kids or the act of falling in love.

My first stop was the police station, a legitimate visit this time, during business hours. I needed to see if all the cops were accounted for and if they had gotten any breaks in the case.

I took the turns widely and slowly, unsure of the Jeep's handling. I had driven a couple different vehicles in the last few days, but I liked none so much as the Buick.

Parking in front of the station, I left the engine running and made sure the doors were unlocked. I didn't want to look the fool by locking myself out.

It was busier inside than I had previously seen it. An elderly couple bundled in scarves and woolen mittens were adjusting and updating notices on the community events board, something about a swap meet and a pageant.

I thought I might have seen them in the restaurant yesterday morning.

No one was at the front desk. No Lang.

The carpets were clean and dark with residual dampness. The fire had not been lit in the pit. Feeling a sense of urgency and a little entitlement given my involvement, I pushed through the door that led to the inner offices.

Rock and French were at their desks.

They had been talking with their feet up but stopped and stood as I entered.

"At ease, guys. No need to stand on my account," I said.

"What do you want?" Rock asked in a way that seemed to suggest he wouldn't volunteer to help.

For a moment I said nothing, debating whether or not to give him a hard time. Mary's voice came to mind though: *You shouldn't have picked on them.*

"Good morning to you too. I need to talk to Chief Strawn," I said.

Like an actor cued onstage, Strawn appeared. "Mr. Sawyer, how can I help you?"

He looked worn, tired. His collar was open, and his sleeves were rolled up. He must have been working hard, although Rock and French seemed unruffled and as lazy as ever.

"I saw the car-thief last night."

He perked up. "Where?"

"Outside Agnes Kirk's house."

"You recovered your vehicle, didn't you?" He seemed genuinely interested.

I looked at Rock, pointedly. "Yes, but when I left to look for Amy with Mary, it was stolen again, right from the restaurant's parking lot."

Rock and French looked confused, which suited them, in my opinion.

"That's two times too many," Strawn said. "I need you to keep your head down and stay clear of this investigation. I seem to recall telling you that before."

I try to err on the side of caution, and being too forthcoming or gung ho can be a very bad idea. As of yet no one had noticed Rock's missing photograph, to my knowledge. Despite my earlier enthusiasm to help out local law enforcement, I was hesitant to shave any more ice off the already-thin layer on which I walked.

"Tell me what happened, then," Strawn said.

So I told him what happened, how I had heard my car and had chased whoever the thieves were from the house but lost them at the end of the road. As I related the encounter, the three cops listened. Strawn looked thoughtful and Rock and French listless.

Strawn continued. "This is the last time I am going to say this: I don't want anything else from you. We've already got two dead bodies."

"Two?" I asked.

He paused, as if he had said too much.

"In addition to the DOA you discovered, we found more remains last night when you saw us at the house. The doctor is examining them now."

He fished in his breast pocket and pulled out a card. "If you see the thief again, call me and don't do anything else, you understand? I'll lock you up if I have to. You can't keep getting lucky against whoever is out there."

"I don't have a cell phone," I said.

"You could use Mary's."

I nodded. "I'll do that."

"Well, we'll get back to work. Thank you for informing us, Mr. Sawyer. We will let you know as soon as we have anything." He lifted his eyes to the door leading to the entrance.

My cue to leave.

Pushing open the door, I saw again the reverse side of Sergeant Lang's desk. There was nothing much of interest besides the hunting photograph. I looked at it again, at the smiling sergeant and his friend, at the dead deer. I hoped Lang hadn't met a similar fate.

People say when you're tired or hungry you're also more creative. Maybe in my case it boosted my recall as well, because there was something familiar in Lang's friend's smiling face. Except when I had seen Lang's friend before, he hadn't been smiling. He had been bruised and bloodied and probably mildly concussed. From our car crash.

He was the driver.

He was the killer.

My blood ran cold, and it had very little to do with the weather. It is a strange thing to have what you consider to be a big question finally answered only to realize that it was just the dagger-tip of a very big iceberg.

I ran through a mental checklist of things I knew, which still wasn't much, and a list of things I didn't know, which was a lot. But I could guess. I was not an expert on divisional rankings, but I figured a police sergeant was fairly senior, like middle-management in a company. So it was possible, even probable, that Lang had been in the department for a long time. He looked to be close to Strawn's age—same generation, anyway.

Maybe Lang's buddy had killed Arlene all those years ago. Maybe he was a psychopath. He had to be, to drive down a highway with a dying man riding shotgun. He had certainly covered their tracks well after killing Arlene, if it had been him, way back when.

But what if Lang was part of it? The pair looked pretty chummy. What if all the police were involved? French's password was persuasive but inconclusive. I couldn't risk revealing this new information, and hadn't Strawn forbidden me from relaying anything else, first after my test drive and then again at Amy's house?

My stomach was growling audibly, and I wanted to pick over the leftovers at Agnes's, but I had more stops to make.

CHAPTER TEN

My first stop was at the residence of one Dr. E. Pike. It took a long time to get there. Mary's Jeep was equipped with GPS and an impressive sound system. I didn't listen to any of her CDs or satellite radio though. When I plugged in the address, the screen brought up a map.

I like maps. A lot. And I can decipher them easily. They just make sense, unlike so many other things. I often think how hard it must have been to be a cartographer before the advent of satellite imagery.

The doctor lived toward the east end of town, close to the farms and fields where I'd first found my Buick. His place was in the middle of a big patch of nothing. No neighbors. It must have been nice.

A barbed-wire fence ran parallel to the road. The driveway was marked by a mailbox shaped like a fish, which made sense since a pike is a kind of freshwater predator. It's also a medieval infantry weapon, but that might have scared away the couriers and the clientele. Better to just stick with the fish.

It was artfully made, in a dynamic pose like it was lunging for a lure, its open, upturned mouth serving as the letter receptacle.

The doctor's house was set way back into his property. There was a metal gate anchored to a wooden fence post. It was open, so I drove right on up a small rise to the house itself. The house was big, built in a rambler style. It wasn't barebones, but it wasn't pretentious or gaudy either.

I was hungry, so I checked the console and the glove compartment for protein or candy bars, mixed nuts, trail mix, or mints. Even some gum would have helped, but there was nothing.

I would try and keep this doctor's visit short and sweet.

Some quack sawbones can be long-winded, which he wasn't. At first.

I knocked and waited and knocked again. I've been known to stand for several minutes at a door because people haven't heard me knock. Maybe my gentle knocking is a subconscious gesture of respect. It's definitely not for fear of breaking the door down, not just by knocking. I'm not that strong.

But I didn't have several minutes to wait right then, so I pushed the glowing circle to the right of the handle with my knuckle. I heard the first four notes of Beethoven's Fifth Symphony, which was a little ominous. It's said to symbolize Fate knocking at the door, which incidentally, I wasn't. I'm not that important.

The doctor came to the door anyway.

He opened it and just looked at me, not angrily, not bewilderedly. Just looked. His white hair and beard were trimmed neatly, and his eyes were bright blue and clear. Normally when someone answers the door, they say *hello* or *yes* like a question. *How may I help you?* and so forth. But the doctor just looked at me, waiting.

It was too late for trick-or-treaters and too early for Christmas carolers.

Still he said nothing, like he was neither surprised nor dismayed by my arrival and wouldn't be at my disappearance either.

"Are you the doctor?" I asked.

"Are you feeling ill?" he asked like he already knew the answer.

"Just hungry."

"Hunger is not a symptom, unless it's significantly increased over a long period of time."

"A few hours is all."

He started to close the door. "Then I would recommend the restaurant."

"I'm not begging for bread here. I can stand the hunger pangs a little while longer. And besides, the café is closed."

He stopped with the door halfway through its range. "You're the miscreant, aren't you? The one who ran from the police?"

"Yes, I am," I said.

"I was in the restaurant yesterday morning. I saw you. Won't you come in?"

So I went in, wiping my boots on the welcome mat.

"I know why you're here," the doctor said.

I said nothing—better just to hear him out.

He continued in what I figured was a doctorly manner— clinically, precisely, his words based on facts.

"You want information. You're helping Miss Agnes and pre- sumably the police."

He looked at me for either a confirmation or a denial.

I gave him neither—better to just hear him out.

"I was also in the restaurant in the evening, when you spoke to Miss Agnes. I am only surprised you didn't come here sooner."

He was not smug or all-knowing—a better doctor than most, probably. I wouldn't know. I have never had to spend much time with medical practitioners. At least he was observant, which is probably a deciding factor between a good physician and a bad one.

"That's about the long and short of it," I said. "And thanks for letting me inside."

"I'm afraid where we're going is not much warmer," he said, leading me farther inside.

"Where's that? Hell?"

He chuckled. He stopped in a spacious sitting room, gesturing at a large bookcase filled with volumes. He asked, "You've read Dante, then?"

In Dante's *Inferno* hell appears as a very cold place, as opposed to the burning lake of fire and brimstone people usually imagine.

He pulled a gold-leafed tome from the shelf.

"No," I said. "Too dreary. I think reading should be fun."

"You can read though?"

"A little."

"My favorite is the second part of the *Divine Comedy*, *Purgatorio*. It discusses how sin is rooted in love; either excessive, deficient, or malicious love leads to evil. Tell me, son, what do you love?"

"A lot of things," I said.

"Name one."

"Boxing."

"Right there, it could be construed that an excessive affinity for a sport leads to envy, of world champions, maybe. Or that malicious love leads to violence. It is a violent pastime, after all. Perhaps, even, it is indicative of a deficiency of love for your neighbor in that you can punch him continually until he is literally rendered unconscious. Dead, in some cases."

His was exactly the kind of overly analytical rhetoric I tried to steer clear of.

But I was in his home, and it was not like he didn't have a slight point. I didn't mention to him that I have gone entire bouts without landing a punch because I don't like hurting people.

"I guess the solution is moderation in everything," I said.

He nodded, replacing the book. "But I digress. Please, follow me."

We left the sitting room, with its old comfortable furniture and hundreds of books. Walking down a wide hallway, we came to an office. There was a computer on a bow-front writing desk. A pair of wooden file cabinets flanked a swivel chair. The desk faced the door and was backed by a wide window. One side wall was bare, and one had a recessed handle. More of a pull, actually, like something you see on a drawer.

The doctor opened the wall with the handle. A hidden door. It swung slowly, heavily, revealing a stairwell.

If he had motioned for me to go first, I might have refused. I don't watch horror movies. I think movies should be fun, and I don't want garbage floating around in my mind. That is why nothing scares me, because I have no pollutants to conjure up demons behind every shadow. But I've seen the headlines from time to time, and it would not have been much of a stretch to imagine the doctor pushing me down the stairs and locking me in a dungeon to starve to death, which I was already well on my way to doing.

But he flipped a switch and started down the stairs. I followed, watching his hands in case he attempted to slice me with a scalpel he had up his sleeve. He didn't.

It did get colder the deeper we went, much colder, like in a meat locker or walk-in freezer.

The staircase dog-legged once, and we came out onto a white-tiled floor. The doctor hit another switch, and fluorescent tubes buzzed to life with much flickering.

We were in a medical examiner's lab. There were big lamps encased in stainless-steel circles over a stainless-steel table. There were stainless-steel scales for weighing things and a stainless-steel sink. There was a drain in the center of the room, a stainless-steel fridge, which seemed unnecessary, and a row of three large stainless-steel lockers. For corpses.

The doctor paused, looking at me. Maybe for effect, maybe to let my non-scientific, non-medical brain connect the dots.

I said nothing—better to just hear him out.

"The chief of police brought this one in himself." He stepped over to the first cadaver drawer and pulled it open.

On the slab was a jumbled collection of charred-black bones.

The doctor went on. "Cluff is limited to volunteer firemen, you understand, as is Troy and much of the entire county. They don't have many resources. They do the best they can, but the house fire was too far along when they arrived. There was no real point in trying too hard to extinguish it because there were no nearby buildings or trees that could have caught, so the police sent them away—"

"Is this normal?" I interrupted.

This time he said nothing, waiting to hear me out.

"To have a makeshift morgue in your basement?" I continued.

"What constitutes normality?" he retorted, not sharply but with a hint of superior wisdom, inviting me to a higher plateau like a college professor. Socratic. Not there to just answer questions but to enlighten the asker.

"Okay, is it *usual?*" I revised.

He shuffled his hands back and forth in a *maybe-maybe-not* gesture. "Perhaps not. But then again, why not? I'm not unaccustomed to mortality, and you certainly haven't vomited yet. I'm old, and this work requires long, irregular hours. It's better if it's close by."

That made some kind of sense.

The doctor continued. "And, of course, violent crimes are exceptionally uncommon here. Most cases are people passing away due to the effects of age, whereupon the funeral parlor in Troy prepares them for burial. I rarely use this lab, and I certainly couldn't afford it were it not for Chief Strawn."

"How's that?"

"In addition to the funeral home, Troy also has the nearest hospital. I only pay house calls on occasion, for minor ailments. But some years ago Chief Strawn offered to keep me on retainer and paid to move the lab from the station to my home."

Which also made sense. It was pretty generous of Strawn, but he seemed to have the budget surplus to spare.

Doctor Pike closed the drawer with the bones, and I was glad of it. I'm not bothered by guts and gore, but I wouldn't want to eat and sleep so close to murder victims.

"Did you know her?" I asked. I didn't want to reveal how much I knew, not yet—better to feign ignorance, play along.

The doctor's eyes sharpened, and he looked at me like I was confused, which I definitely was.

He pulled open the bone drawer again. "*These* are not the bones of a woman."

CHAPTER ELEVEN

"What?" I looked from the doctor to the bones.

"These bones don't belong to a female," he repeated, slower.

"I heard you," I said. "So where is Amy?"

"That is a question for the police. Though I have yet to inform them of my findings, so *they* don't even know this isn't her. Chief Strawn made the same incorrect assumption when he brought the remains to me as you did. I was going to call him and then Agnes. Then I saw you driving young Mary's vehicle, and I expected you were coming for answers on her behalf."

"Doctor, can you hold off on breaking this news to anyone, please?"

Like he was auditioning for the part of Hamlet, he held up the skull. It looked brittle; it had already begun to crack. There was a hole in the forehead the size of my little finger.

"Why should I do that, young man?" He indicated the hole and then turned the skull around to where there was a bigger hole. "This is where the bullet exited. I am not a ballistics expert by any means, but if I had to hazard a guess, which is what most science is, I would say it was caused by a 9-mm bullet. This is something the police will want to know."

I hesitated. "Doctor, I believe there is something nefarious in the police force. I don't know whom we can trust at the moment."

He paused and looked at me like I was a student asking permission for the bathroom. "Such has been my hypothesis. I can wait, perhaps," he said.

I nodded. I had a couple more questions. "Did you know Arlene Kirk?" I asked.

"Yes, I did. I have been here a long time."

"What did you think when she was killed?"

He blinked, set the skull down gently, and looked at me. "I don't know that I *thought* anything. Thoughts have absolutely no influence on facts. And the *fact* is that her death was a tragedy and entirely unnecessary. I wish I had been there."

"Because you could have saved her?" I said.

"Seattle is well-known for having good doctors and better nurses, particularly at the Children's Hospital. I don't know that I am much better, but being personally invested can lend significant strength. It can, of course, also compromise one's reason. I like to think I could have done something differently, something better, but the past is the past, and I cannot change it. In such cases doctors often choose the mother over the infant—a terrible choice—but as I understand it, Arlene was beyond saving."

"She gave her life for her baby," I said.

"A courageous woman. It was what any woman would do, I wish I could say, but we live in a time in which women kill babies instead and think themselves brave for it or entitled to it."

I liked the doctor.

"Any idea who did it?"

"Again, that is a job for the police. Forensics weren't what they are now. I wasn't there."

I nodded. It had been twenty-five years ago. "But you might have had an idea?" I asked, hopefully, desperately, really, for any clue.

The doctor answered, "If I had to guess, which as I said, is only half of the scientific process, I would say it was either a weak man who lost control or a strong man who exercised it."

"How do you figure?"

"It was a man, certainly, because it usually is. And he was either a weak man because he was not able to kill her, not immediately, that is. I suspect the weak man because a stronger attacker likely would have killed her with one blow to the head. But there was no uniformity to the wounds, which seems to eliminate any degree of control or precision."

"One more question, Doc."

He held up a hand. "You're going to ask me why I am being so forthcoming in matters of an ongoing investigation, with a complete stranger at that. My answer is this: I seek righteousness, Mr. Sawyer. And you are helping Agnes. And she is my friend, so what is good enough for her is good enough for me."

"Actually I was going to ask something else, but thank you, Doctor, for the vote of confidence. I was going to ask if you know everyone in town."

"I try to provide care and compassion to everybody, but there are those who prefer berries and poultices and vinegar. Home remedies, in short."

"Do you know where Chief Strawn lives?"

He gave me the address, and I thanked him. Then he asked me to keep him informed, and I said I would. We came back up to the warm main level, and he saw me to the door. As we stood in the entryway the doctor put a hand on my shoulder. "Young man, be careful. I expect you can handle yourself, but there is a cold-blooded killer on the loose."

"I'll be careful," I lied.

"And be careful with Officer Roca. I don't presume to know the particulars of your feud with him, but it was evident at the restaurant. Be advised he was sent for SWAT training in Helena, if I am not mistaken."

I nodded, walked back to the Jeep, and drove away, my hunger moving once again to the back burner. I was happy to be out of the morgue.

I drove Mary's Jeep through the snow, glancing from the road to the screen and back again, until I came to Cluff's inner ring and found the turn onto the seven o'clock spoke.

I found Strawn's place; it was a nice piece of property with plenty of acreage. A house, a shed, and a barn were set in a loose triangle, each about a hundred yards from the other. No cars were parked out front, and I figured Strawn was still working. There was no mailbox demarking the driveway. Just a fence that stopped and started at either side of the entrance. There was no smoke rising from the brick chimney, which assured me further that nobody was home. It was still snowing heavily, like powdered sugar on pancakes. It looked like it would keep snowing forever. There was plenty of fresh powder obscuring the earth. There were no fresh tracks anywhere in sight, so I decided to just walk right up to the house like I was just some guy asking for directions or a salesman or a missionary.

The house itself was a one-story ranch with a two-car garage bumped out on the side, not brand-new, not dilapidated. The paint on the siding and the shingles on the roof were old but looked to be mostly maintained, as did the outbuildings.

Trudging through the snow, I stopped between the house and the shed, listening. Nothing.

I looked at the barn. It was dormant and still, under a load of snow.

I went back to the house.

The front door was locked.

Maybe there was a spare key. I felt along the lintel. Nothing. I looked under the mat. Still nothing.

Most people do not look up. Maybe it is an evolutionary thing. Most dangers come from below—snakes and pits and stumbling blocks. It's not like people walk around worrying about pterodactyls carrying them away.

So I guessed a spare key would be up high, somewhere likely to not be immediately recognized as a logical place but still accessible on the off chance of Strawn being locked out in a storm.

I went back down to the shed and felt the top of the door. Nothing.

The shed was unlocked, so I stepped inside.

It was much like Agnes's shed but a little better stocked, a little better used, and a little more meticulous. It was dusty though. I looked through some drawers and cans and panned through some trays of screws and nails.

I was beginning to think maybe the chief didn't have a spare key.

On the wall were some fishing trophies mounted on plaques. None of them compared to the giant arapaima in Peru, but they were all right. I recognized several smallmouth bass, a trout, a walleye, and a northern pike. It made me think of the doctor. All the fish were crafted to be turned, slightly open-mouthed, toward me, but the walleye was angled up, its pose reminiscent of Dr. Pike's mailbox.

I had an idea.

I stepped around some boxes and went to the fish. When I turned it upside down, a little brass key fell out.

Bingo.

I went and unlocked the door to the house and then hustled back to the shed, replacing the key. It was a clever spot, and I was sure that without some inspiration, I never would have thought to look there.

Returning to the house, I stepped inside. It was clean and organized—cold, without a fire burning on the hearth, but neat and tidy. There were no dirty dishes in the sink, no stains or gouges in the hardwood floor or furniture. Everything was all squared away in a comfortable, unpretentious manner that almost beguiled me into kindling a blaze and waiting patiently for the master of the house to arrive so we might sit down together and talk.

But I didn't do that, because I suspected I might be standing in the home of an accessory to murder. Maybe.

I started searching, not really with anything in mind—just a fool's hope of finding something to set me on the right course. I opened the drawers in the kitchen. There were dish towels and utensils, assorted teas, and sandwich bags. One drawer was filled with loose batteries, tape, rubber bands, screwdrivers, and other hand tools that might be needed on a regular basis—a utility drawer. Growing up, my family had such a drawer. We called it the *futility* drawer because we could never find exactly what we were looking for.

There were no antlers hanging on the walls, which surprised me, given the station's decor. Maybe he was more of a subsistence hunter. I checked the freezer and found plenty of packaged venison.

I moved on through the house. Nothing jumped out at me, literally or figuratively.

I stayed in the middle of rooms, moving fast around corners so I couldn't be blindsided if someone was lying in wait. Nothing caught my interest. Nothing stood out. There was a glass case with a couple shotguns and rifles. The bed was made, and no one was hiding underneath it. On the dresser I came across a giant leather-bound photo album. I brought it with me into the living room, sat down like I owned the place, and flipped through the pages. I once heard someone more cynical than me describe photo albums as journals for illiterate people, which I disagree with. I think journals and photographs are both essential. *A picture is worth a thousand words* and all that. And words, well-crafted, paint the prettiest pictures. So, all in all, I think words and pictures come out just about evenly.

That is when I realized I wasn't alone.

CHAPTER TWELVE

A HUGE, BLACK, FURRY MASS, impossibly large, loomed out of the shadows behind a recliner.

I thought it was a wolf, but it was too big. Or maybe a bear, but it wasn't quite big enough.

A dog. I like dogs a lot. But contrary to General Woundwort's assertions in Richard Adams's *Watership Down*, dogs can be dangerous.

This one was big enough to rip my throat out or crush me. It probably weighed as much as I did and had much sharper teeth.

I was rooted to the spot with surprise and could not have dodged if I had wanted to. But the huge dog didn't charge, didn't bark or snarl or foam at the mouth, didn't even whimper or whine. He just trundled slowly, like a giant tortoise, until he came and rested his massive head on my leg and looked at me with sad puppy-dog eyes out of an old dog's face.

I patted the dog's head. He—I assumed it was a he, given his size—closed his eyes and wagged his tail. He was a behemoth. I would have pegged him at seven feet, from nose to tail. I thought this dog must have been hungry, since Strawn seemed to spend so much time out. I stood up, brushing drool and dog hair from my pants. The gentle giant had some degree of limited movement, maybe arthritis or plain ancient age, but when I stood up he sensed food and started bucking and rocking like a horse. He tossed his head and panted and tried to rear, only lifting his front paws a hairsbreadth off the floor. He started off through the house, and I followed until he stopped in a type of mudroom with an old name-brand washer and dryer set.

Nudging a pair of bowls with his nose, the dog looked at me expectantly, hungrily. There was a deep farm sink between the dryer and a door that had been propped open leading into the garage. I filled one bowl with water and had barely set it down before he was slopping it over the floor.

I looked in the garage and found a doggy door that led outside. There were no cars but plenty of junk: fishing gear, sports equipment, some more tools, clay pigeons for target practice. I found a big plastic trash bin full of dry dog food. It looked pretty much the same as most box cereals nowadays, except it smelled more savory.

The big dog was lapping up the last of the water. Poor guy. Going hungry is one thing, but going thirsty is worse.

I refilled the water bowl and then grabbed the one for food. Scooping up a portion from the bin in the garage, I noticed stenciled lettering on the curved face. *MAX*. Max the dog. Not very original, but extremely accurate, given his size. If dogs had surnames, I would have suggested *Power*. Max Power, like a setting on a blender or a hair dryer.

He slaked his thirst before moving to the food.

I was hungry. Not so hungry that I was going to eat dog food.

Patting Max on the shoulder, I wandered back into the kitchen. Scrounging like a raccoon, I found a cast-iron skillet, a carton of eggs, and thick-cut bacon.

I turned on the stove, and it hissed and clicked to life as the gas caught fire. Then I adjusted the flame and set the skillet to warm. I am no gourmet, but I get by all right. Cooking is like anything—an application of correct principles with plenty of room for improvisation.

Max ambled back in and flumped onto the floor with an audible expulsion of air.

"Good boy," I said. And he was.

I think he sensed I was a friend. I like dogs. A lot.

The bacon sizzled and popped, and the eggs were big and scrambled nicely. They weren't store-bought—probably from a neighbor's coop judging by the lack of uniformity. I felt bad about the detour, wanting to find Amy as soon as I could, but I figured I would not be of much use to anyone if I fainted from lack of food. And besides, someone had to take care of Max. Switching the stove off, I tossed a couple of slices of bacon to the floor for Max. He scooted and inched like an elephant seal until he got close enough to get his teeth on it.

"Careful," I said. "It's hot."

I ate out of the pan to spare any extra dishes and set everything in the sink. Then I left.

I closed the door behind me, carrying the photo album. Lang's picture had given me the biggest clue so far, so I figured I might as well peruse Strawn's mementos.

Lang's house was next. It took me closer to the station. I hoped everyone was busy and wouldn't happen upon me snooping. Lang's house was the most central of all my stops so far but was still at the end of its own street, the six o'clock spoke. No neighbors there either.

The road was narrow, and a sign advised me it was a dead end, which was not encouraging, in a literal sense. But I didn't take it that way. I am an optimist, after all.

I didn't know what I would find. Maybe nothing.

I passed the house slowly. There was a snow-covered pickup truck nose out in the driveway. It looked like the civilian version of Lang's police vehicle. It had all trappings too: mag wheels, running boards, a lift kit, and upgraded headlights. There was also a lump of snow on a stick, which might have been a mailbox. The house was a single-story with an attached garage. No lights were on. I turned around and parked. Climbing out, I looked around. Afternoon had worn on steadily to evening, and the clouds and mountains made everything darker.

There were no signs of life. No lamps. No blue glow from a television or computer screen. No sounds.

I climbed a set of steps to an uncovered porch, carrying the photo album with me. I would rather look through it inside than in the Jeep. Anyone could sneak up on me seated in a vehicle. A security light above the garage came on, but that was it. The front door paint was peeling, and the door looked old. I was pretty sure I could have kicked it down.

But maybe I wouldn't need to. The top third of the door was mostly comprised of a window, which people forget to lock sometimes.

I set the album down.

Since the lip for lifting the window was on the inside, I had to press my palms against the cold glass and push in and up to keep the tension. I was careful not to put my hands straight through. The window gave, stuck, and then came up some more. When I got it far enough to wedge my fingers under, I pried it up, slipped my forearm in, reached the lock, and opened the door from the inside.

I didn't expect anyone to be home. It was dark inside. And cold. But anything was warmer than outside.

Listening intently, I closed my eyes to heighten my hearing. Nothing. Maybe a faint squeak, like a mouse or a bedspring. But I couldn't be sure. It was hard to tiptoe in boots, but I managed to walk mostly silently. *Heel, toe, heel, toe.*

Bumping into what felt like a leather armchair, I held my breath in case the noise alerted any as yet undetected occupants.

Nothing.

Leaving the album on the chair, I kept moving, even slower this time. Reaching out like a blind man for balance, I felt the grainy walls. I resisted the impulse to hit a light switch my finger traced. Only the blind or the very, very brave are comfortable in darkness. I actually don't mind the dark, but I can't abide the cold. Nobody likes the cold. People who say they do actually mean they like being able to transition instantly from winter wonderlands into the balmy comfort of roofs and walls with insulation and furnaces and cocoa.

The drapes were drawn on all the windows so only a sliver of dying sunlight seeped in where the folds didn't quite meet. I kept listening and heard nothing. Every muscle and tendon screamed for silence as I crept forward. Everything seems loud when you're trying to move furtively. Even the carpet seemed crunchy.

But there was no sound.

I paused again and listened, stretching my senses for any of the tiny vibrations people give off. Lots of people can sense when they are not alone or being watched. I didn't get that sensation right then. Now I was sure no one was home. But there was something, like a hum.

I continued with my arms out in front of me like a mummy or a zombie. Except I was alive, which is how I wanted to stay. Technically I was an intruder. But my intentions were honest. Not that good intentions are much of a defense against bullets or lawsuits.

The kitchen was the next room off the front. It was slightly better illuminated by the reflective surfaces of stainless-steel appliances and an uncovered window above the sink. I could make out the shape of plates stacked on the countertops. It smelled like burned coffee and onions.

Delicious.

The linoleum must have been old and unwashed. It was sticky, and my boots made peeling noises with each step. So I stretched my stride to shorten the journey. Beyond the kitchen was a narrow hallway like the one in Agnes's house. I didn't think Lang would have been the type to hang portraits and needlepoints on the wall, but you never know, so I kept my hands low as I felt along the walls so as not to knock anything down. Nobody hangs things at hip height.

The house was small. The darkness and the cold made it feel uncomfortably cramped. I realized that during my whole caper, I hadn't considered the possibility of Lang having a dog as well, which he didn't, thankfully. I had seen plenty of them during the last two years. In Peru there are thousands of stray dogs. Some form packs. Most have mange. They'd been known to bite missionaries, but they'd never bothered me. They're man's best friend, after all. I had two Labrador retrievers as a kid. Maybe the dogs in Peru had sensed I was a friend and unafraid, like Max had.

My left-hand fingertips grazed a doorknob, maybe of a bathroom. Most houses situated the bedrooms farthest from the front door, so I suspected the closed door at the end of the hall must have been to a bedroom.

I was facing the door directly, so I opened it and found nothing but an empty bedroom. I kept searching, not knowing exactly what I might find. I risked turning on some lights for a minute to see if anything had escaped my initial inspection. The house furnishings were pretty skeletal—no knickknacks, no junk—but it was dirty with neglect. All he had was the armchair I had bumped into, a couch, and a coffee table. Both the couch and chair were aimed at a monstrous flat screen television. There were dust bunnies and cobwebs on all the edges.

I figured Lang lived alone. No self-respecting woman would let Lang get away with an unvacuumed and dirty living space. He was a hunter, so he had to have gear and guns. I didn't see anything in the hallway, bedroom, or entryway closets, so his stuff had to be in the garage.

I turned off the house lights and felt my way through the hallway to another door close to the bathroom. It opened to the garage. Feeling around, I found a switch that ignited a row of fluorescent lights. Below the switch was a button I guessed opened the garage door. There were all sorts of tools on pegs and a workbench with an electric saw and drill. There was a gun safe, big enough for a dozen rifles, and there were plenty of antlers from deer, elk, other members of the *Cervidae* genus, and some exotic specimens.

There was a car, too, covered with a tarp, and water from melted snow all around suggested it had been driven recently, which made me wonder how many cars Lang had. His pickup was out in the snow, and of course, he wasn't here, so he must have had another car, but I would have figured he mostly drove his department-issued vehicle. I pulled the tarp off to get a look at his ride; It must have been a nice one for him to leave his fancy truck outside in the snow.

It was a white Mercury Grand Marquis. Amy's car.

Not good.

Now I knew for sure Lang was in on Amy's disappearance. Had he started the fire? Where was Amy?

Continuing my scouring of the garage, I inspected the slab floor. Most of the place was covered in sawdust and metal shavings. On the wall nearest the door to the house was a row of lockers like what you see in a gym or school. There were six total. Each was unlocked, and each held a different set of hunting clothing, camouflage, and reflective orange. Each seemed geared for a different season or different terrain. The only empty one was the last, and the only missing color was white. His winter camouflage, gone. Not a pleasant thought. What would he be hunting at night in the dead of winter?

I looked around a little more and saw that while the floor was mostly clean, it was not unmarked. There was a thin scrape that ran in a perfect arc from the edge of the row of lockers, like it had been dragged across the floor. The arc was uniform, though, a perfect partial circle. I squatted down. The mark was smooth, like whoever had made it had tried to buff it out. I traced it back to the base of the lockers. Looking at the lockers again, I saw hinges welded on one side. I grabbed the other end and tugged. The entire bank of lockers swung open fairly easily. The hinges were well-oiled, but the bottom corner screeched and ground slightly against the garage floor. I didn't open the secret door the full length of its trajectory, just enough so I could slide into the hidden room. The buzzing I had sensed earlier intensified like a thousand flies around a trash pile.

Inside was not a particularly large room, but it was warm, probably insulated for heat or sound or both. There was a loud hum from motors and stacks of computer equipment I couldn't have made heads or tails of. It was all far more sophisticated than what I had seen at the station—way more than you would need to connect to FaceChat or Snapbook or InstaTweet. A black box as tall as I was buzzed and blinked with green lights. On a low table was a bank of blank monitors. Stacks of CDs or DVDs rested on the edge, and on a plastic shelf were boxes of miniature cameras and devices.

I hit the spacebar on a wireless keyboard, and the middle monitor sprang to life. It didn't require a password.

I was unsure where to click or what to do because the screen was blank and blue.

But then something happened. One of the other monitors blinked into activity, and a smaller window appeared. It showed a scene I was familiar with, showed a *person* I was familiar with: Mary. In her bathroom.

The hidden camera must have been small but expensive. The quality of the feed wasn't the worst I had ever seen, but it wasn't high definition. A banner on the top right of the window indicated a live stream, and there was a steady flow of viewers that seemed to be increasing, like in some sort of chatroom. Weird usernames and off-color comments appeared, accompanied by little pictures created from numbers and shapes and symbols. I ground my teeth. Mary brushed hers. It was relatively early, so she wasn't getting ready for bed. Maybe she was a compulsive dental hygienist. Another monitor blipped into action and showed some electronic transactions, money being deposited into an account.

Lang was supplementing his income by the seediest of means.

I was angry. I liked Mary a lot. And it incensed me to know she was being seen in her most private moments by perverts across the globe. I found a yellow cable connected to a tower unit under the table and pulled it out. An error message popped up and advised me that Internet connectivity was lost. The camera feed did not stop, though, maybe due to a separate wireless connection. I didn't want to see anything Mary wouldn't want me to, so I moved a wireless mouse until the arrow came into view, and I found an icon to minimize the window.

My face was hot. I'm not a prude, but I have standards and scruples, and I felt angry and a little embarrassed. I didn't know how I would tell her about this development in the case. What reason would she have to believe I hadn't watched her? I figured I would burn that bridge when I came to it.

Periodically other windows popped up, showing feeds from more hidden cameras. They appeared to be motion-activated. I closed out each in turn.

I laughed darkly to myself at the idea that some freaks had logged on last night in the hopes of seeing Mary and had instead seen me showering—an unpleasant surprise. There is nothing provocative about me.

I clicked around the screen until I found an icon of a file folder. I opened it, squinting my eyes to blur my vision just in case there was something I didn't want to see, but it was safe. There were just file names. Some were starred. Each was listed by last name, first name, and date. I found a search window and looked for *Kirk*. I found several files for Amy and Agnes.

I clicked on the most recently uploaded file. I did the squinty thing with my eyes again, just in case something sensitive popped up. It didn't. In fact, the file showed a variety of angles from a variety of rooms. Amy's house. None of the feeds indicated a live stream, and the cameras were rolling without being activated by movement.

Like French, maybe Lang was weirdly obsessed with Amy. I could see why he might have been as soon as she came into view. She was quite simply the most beautiful girl I had ever seen.

She was like Helen of Troy, whose face launched a thousand ships. Amy had, through no fault of her own and by simply being beautiful, incited a war.

She was tall, blonde, lithe, and perfectly proportioned. She was in sweatpants and a T-shirt but couldn't have looked any more spectacular in a designer dress. She moved around the house like a dream; even while performing routine tasks she looked elfin.

Mary was right up there with her in terms of beauty, just in a different way. She was strong where Amy was delicate, soft where Amy looked firm. It was the difference between green pastures in Ireland and sculptures in the Louvre, beautiful and matchless in completely different ways.

I scrolled through the recording until something changed. Amy stood up from a bowl of soup and opened her front door. Three people stood on her step. I recognized two of them: Lang and the dead FBI guy from the car. The third guy was also an agent. He and his partner showed their badges. Lang was in uniform, and Amy knew him, presumably. She shook their hands and showed them in. Lang looked directly at the cameras. The four of them sat down in the living room.

It reminded me of my missionary service. *We'd like to share a message with you.*

Then the other agent, the one who hadn't been in the car, stood up and asked Amy something, maybe for the bathroom. Amy pointed, and he went down the hallway to the restroom. From a different camera angle I saw him as he looked at himself in the mirror and then turned and stopped. He looked up, noticing something. The camera. He looked right into the lens, put his fingers to it, and pulled it. That feed died. Another angle picked him up returning to the living room. He held up the camera.

His partner stood up.

Amy stood up.

Lang stood up. And shot the FBI agents. He was quick, like a western gunslinger.

The video screen whited out with each muzzle flash. There was no sound, but I was sure Amy was screaming. Lang stepped in and grabbed her roughly. I had misjudged her. I had taken her for delicate, but she didn't wilt like a flower. She fought like a lioness. She clawed and kicked and bit at Lang, but he was strong and backhanded her across the mouth. She fell and tried to get back up, but Lang kicked her in the head.

She was unconscious.

Lang bent down and grabbed Amy by the heels and began dragging her to the door.

Then something else happened. The door opened, and before Lang could straighten back up, he himself was knocked unconscious with the butt of a rifle, wielded by none other than the driver who had hit me over the head. He seemed to have a propensity for thumping people on the cranium.

He lifted Amy up in his arms and carried her out. A moment later he came back inside and checked the FBI guy who had found the camera. Dead. But the driver found a set of car keys. Then he turned and noticed the other agent, who was still alive but only just. He half-carried, half-dragged him out.

So he wasn't a bad guy. And he was no friend of Lang's, not anymore. But what had he been doing there?

I fast-forwarded the video until Lang stirred and stood, shaking his head. He looked around and stomped about. He seemed angry and unsure as to what to do next. He left and came back in, started digging around, took something from a drawer, and left again. Nothing else happened on the video. I scrolled along the timeline. The only changes were in the lighting. Darkness came, and the camera adjusted to a greenish gray—a ghostly, washed-out, illuminated view. I kept scrolling, and then the next day dawned. The light changed, and the shadows moved. Eventually Lang came back, this time in his policeman's uniform. He carried a can of gasoline, sloshing it all around. He poured plenty over the dead agent and left a trail out the door, and a minute later fire spread along the gasoline path, licking its way up the walls. Soon the whole place ignited. The flames spread, the brightness whiting out my view, and soon the video died.

So Amy was alive and presumably safe, which meant her savior wasn't out to kill Agnes.

But then, why had he run from me at Agnes's house?

And what had the FBI been doing there with Lang in the first place? What was Strawn's hand in all of this, if any?

I didn't think the computer could give me any more insight, so I unplugged everything and resisted the urge to smash it all to pieces.

I felt sick. I had just witnessed two people shot to death and had stumbled upon an evil enterprise. At least Amy was alive. For now.

Prayer is not magic. There is no such thing as magic. It's not like rubbing a lamp to conjure a genie. It's not casting spells with rote incantations. There is no hocus pocus. Prayer is, however, an expression of the soul's most sincere desires. Some people have decried prayer as a form of begging, but it isn't that either.

I've prayed a lot in my life, for all sorts of things. And I'm happy to say, God has given me everything I've ever asked for, which sounds nice, but I've always tried to be humble in prayer.

God might not give everybody what they want or what they deserve, which is good, because I deserve much worse than what I've got. But He always gives people what they need.

Prayer doesn't necessitate closing eyes, folding arms, or kneeling. That certainly helps eliminate distractions, but you can pray anywhere and any way.

Right then I certainly was praying. Hard. All I could think was, *God, help me.* Not because I was scared—I wasn't—but because I wanted to fight crime. I wanted to break every bone in Lang's body.

But he was armed. He was a police officer, after all. He had looked like he would have shot me when we first met. That certainly would have saved him and me some trouble. Not that I was overly eager to die, but I wasn't planning on making a big deal about it when the time came.

I exited the hidden room and breathed more easily. The garage itself was a lot colder; it was refreshing.

Then I heard a car's engine rumbling along. Not my Buick. Who was behind the wheel? Lang?

Not good.

He would see the Jeep.

I wouldn't get the chance to surprise him. Hustling back into the house, I peered out the gap in the curtains without moving them and without pressing my face up against them. The way to look out a window without showing yourself is to stay well back in the room. With the lights off inside, it is even better. You can see from a dark place into a light place but not from a light place into a dark place.

It was Rock and French.

I sat in the armchair, made myself comfortable, and waited.

I closed my eyes. Whenever you expect a drastic change of illumination, you should close your eyes until after the change. It helps your eyes adjust quicker.

They knocked on the door. I heard them talking. They waited but got impatient and tried the handle. It opened.

"Lang?" Rock called. "Where are you? What's Mary's Jeep doing here?"

They found the light switch and flipped it.

I stayed seated but raised my hands to show them I was unarmed. "Welcome," I said. It sounded lame.

They stopped, reeling back in surprise, but they recovered fairly quickly.

Rock spoke first. "What the devil are you doing here?"

"Same as you—trying to catch a criminal," I said.

They came into the living room. I sat, looking at the album on the low coffee table, trying to look as nonthreatening as possible.

"We might have just caught one," Rock said. "You're breaking and entering."

"Not at the moment. And maybe it was open when I got here."

"Doesn't matter," French said. "We're taking you in. We just came to see where Lang is, and here we find you sneaking around."

I just sat there and waited for them to make the first move, which I don't often recommend. It is a good standard practice to not let someone else keep their own timetable. You want to mess up the narrative they have in their head, ideally by busting them in the head. But they seemed in no great hurry to start something, so I just sat there.

"Sit down, guys; let's be civilized. We're on the same side, I hope."

They sat side by side on the couch, which was a plus, since there is no quick way to draw a gun from your hip when you're sitting in a soft sofa, with your knees higher than your waist.

"I thought Chief wanted you to butt out," Rock said.

"He did, but I kind of got swept back in. Credit is all yours, though, once we solve this thing. I just want to get my car and get out of town."

Rock looked like he might have been genuinely pacified toward me until he remembered something. "What are you doing driving Mary's car?"

"She let me borrow it."

He glowered. "You'd better leave her alone. We should just arrest you for B and E and car theft too."

"You really shouldn't," I said flatly, not like I was begging him or anything, not like I was scared—just like it would be mutually beneficial to avoid all the hassle.

"Why's that?" Rock asked.

"Because I have new information," I said.

"About what?" French asked.

"What can you tell me about Amy Kirk?" I asked.

French folded his hands, shifting his impressive weight.

"She's dead. We found her body, burned in her house," Rock said.

I shook my head. "I just talked to the doctor. Those bones weren't hers. They were another FBI guy, like the one I found at the crash. And there's video proof of the bad guy. It's Lang."

They exchanged glances.

French asked, "Really?"

"You bet," I said. "So let's help each other. Let's help Amy. Her car is in the garage right here, along with the footage."

"I guess you could help; you've gotten further than us, anyway," Rock said.

I nodded.

Rock nodded, too, like he was seeing the light. I hadn't expected such a quick conversion.

We all stood up slowly, in a truce, an alliance, really. Truces are temporary. I didn't want any more problems with them.

I remembered Mary. *You shouldn't have picked on them.*

"Where do we start?" I asked.

But whatever local knowledge and support they were about to impart was cut short by a crackle of static from the radio on Rock's left shoulder.

The voice came through a little garbled and muted, but there was no mistaking whose it was—Strawn's.

"What's going on?"

Rock crossed his right hand to his left shoulder and pressed a button. The motion made his bicep bulge through his uniform.

He looked at me. "Sawyer's here."

More static. The voice, garbled and muted, said, "Arrest him."

We all looked at each other, the truce broken, alliance null.

Then we all started moving, pretty much simultaneously. I could see French's hesitancy and Rock's indecisiveness plainly on their faces. French didn't look like he was in love with the idea of arresting me again, and Rock looked like he couldn't make his mind up about what to grab first: his gun, his handcuffs, or me. It gave me a split-second's advantage.

I remembered Mary. *You shouldn't pick on them.*

But they were picking on me.

I wanted to throw the entire table at them, but I couldn't hoist it and hurl it fast enough, so I opted for the photo album, which was substantial enough to slow them down a little. French was the lesser of the two evils and the smaller threat, but he was more in line for the tactical album strike. So I grabbed it by a corner and flung it like a Frisbee, hitting him in the face and sending four-by-ten photographs all over the place, like confetti at a New Year's Eve party.

Rock, by this time, was well on his way to catching up, forgetting his gear in favor of getting ahold of me. I went to boxing basics. *Don't back up*—your attacker can always move faster forward than you can backward—so I made it easy on Rock and dove at him, tumbling over the armchair and knocking it down. We got tangled up in a weird embrace, like we were the best of friends, reunited at long last. My sudden lunge took him off-balance, and we toppled over, tipping the couch over onto its back in our fall.

Rock was bigger than me, a distinct advantage on the ground, especially with reinforcements close at hand. If he had gotten on top of me, it would have been over, but we stayed on our sides, still tangled up in a horizontal replica of our vertical bear hug. There is really no good way to hit someone while lying down on your side, but there is really no bad way either. So I just lashed out, smacking him in the face and head while I flailed and wiggled away. I scrambled back to my feet and checked on French to see if he needed further persuading to stay out of it.

He didn't. He was holding his hand over an eye and bleeding from his nose, which I thought was a bit of an overreaction, but some guys bleed easily. Maybe he had gotten hit with a hard corner.

I didn't care.

Rock was coming back to his feet and dropping a hand to his belt. Not good. Or *very* good, as it turned out. Because even though Rock was about to unholster a fight-ending trump card, he sacrificed his shield to do it. As soon as his hand was down, his chin was wide open and unprotected. I snapped a short left hook that sent spit from his mouth and then cracked his jaw shut with a right uppercut. He staggered but stayed on his feet.

He shook his head and came right back at me. He faked an overhand right and came in with a left hook. I ducked underneath and smashed a right to his kidney, using the energy from that punch to spin off, getting a better angle on him. He grunted and swung a quick right at me that glanced off the top of my skull. The punch sent a ringing through my head. It hurt; that was for sure. I straightened up fast, fetching him a right uppercut to the chin again. As his head snapped back, I launched a jab that turned into a left elbow to his right temple. Rocking backward, he bounced off the wall. He was big and strong, but the lights were going out upstairs. I helped him along by skipping forward and rocking a head-butt to the center of his face. That did the trick. Like biting into a farm-fresh carrot, there was a satisfying crunch.

He sank to his knees and fell face-first onto the floor. I checked on French, who was backed up against the wall, just trying to stay as far out of the way as possible. He was holding his nose and stumbling around. He bumped the television, and it wobbled unsteadily. I watched as it tipped onto its face just like Rock and crashed down with another satisfying crunch.

French stepped back from the broken appliance, leaning forward with his hands on his head like he was nursing a migraine. I rolled Rock onto his side, positioning him between the fallen couch and the wall. His nose looked bad and was swelling fast. Corners of his mouth had blood in them, but he would live, no doubt about that. I relieved him of his pistol, putting the two spare magazines into my pocket where they clicked and clinked together. I kept hold of the pistol in case I needed to keep French compliant. But he just looked up at me, blinking.

"What did you throw that book at me for?"

I motioned with my head to Rock. "So I didn't have to do *that* to you."

He said nothing.

"You want me to?" I asked.

"No."

"Then stand up."

He stood.

"Turn around."

He turned.

I helped myself to his sidearm and ammunition as well, stuffing them into my pockets until I must have looked like Rambo.

"Now, handcuff Rock."

He frowned at me but didn't argue. He didn't seem to have any stomach for a fight, which was fine with me. My knuckles were a little sore from Rock's hard face, and the head-butt had brought back echoes of my old headache. You have to be careful punching things without wearing gloves. Hands are very, very fragile. But Rock had only needed a couple combinations. Elbows are usually the way to go but I hadn't wanted him too badly damaged. All's well that ends well.

He snicked the cuffs on less tightly than I would have. Some drops of blood fell onto Rock's inert form. I motioned with the gun for French to sit down, making sure to keep my index finger well away from the trigger. I didn't want to shoot anyone.

He sat down heavily, still blinking, still bleeding. Looking up at me, he asked, "Have you ever been in love?"

"Not with you, not even close," I said.

"No, I mean like with a girl."

"Once upon a time," I said.

"Me too," he said, pushing a toe through the fallen photos.

"Good to know," I said.

"With Amy, man."

That got my attention. I lowered the gun.

He continued. "In high school, I got called names. It made me want to be a cop. I don't like bullies." I frowned and gestured from him to Rock and back to him.

"I know, I know," he said. "But it wasn't always like that. Amy was nice to me. From the day I met her I was head over heels for her. When kids took my sandwiches, she would share."

"Did your love go unrequited?" I asked.

"What's that mean?"

"Did she love you back?" I asked.

"I don't think so, not so you'd notice, anyway. But we were friends."

"A couple of questions," I said. "What do you think happened to her?"

"All I know is she's in trouble. I thought she was dead, and then you told me she's alive, so I got real hopeful. That's why I didn't mess with you. I don't want you locked up. I want you to find her. You didn't have to throw anything at me."

He was starting to make me feel bad, like I was one of the schoolyard tough guys that took his lunch.

"I'm sorry," I said, and I meant it. "So all that before was just playacting?"

He shrugged. "Strawn told us to ride you pretty hard, make you feel unwelcome, stuff like that."

"Did you know about her mother?" I asked.

"Not until just recently. She never talked about her mom, and I never asked. Too shy. I never really said much of anything. I got all tongue-tied. But when you showed up, Strawn got really agitated, angry almost, but more worried. I had never seen him like that."

"Where did Strawn come from?"

"I don't know."

But I didn't need to ask. All I had to do was look down. There were old photographs everywhere, and newspaper clippings. I fished one off the floor and looked at it more closely. The color was fading with age, but it wasn't a good photo to begin with.

Poor lighting. It was of a young Strawn with his arm around Amy. No, not Amy. Arlene. They were almost identical.

CHAPTER THIRTEEN

"He's Amy's father," I said.

French looked at me. His eye looked okay; there was some discoloration around the edges but no permanent damage. His nose had stopped bleeding.

"What do you mean?"

I handed him the photograph.

"They look alike," he said.

"It's an uncanny resemblance. I think Strawn is Arlene's murderer, and I think he sent Lang to kill Amy. The FBI was at Amy's; now they're dead. The guy in the photo on Lang's desk saved her."

"In the picture with Lang? That's Patton. Ross Patton. He lives in a cabin somewhere; I don't know where. He's kind of solitary, except he takes us hunting sometimes. So Lang burned down the house?"

"He had hidden cameras all over the place in Amy's house and Mary's—all the pretty girls' houses, I'm sure," I said.

French blushed. "We have to stop them."

"We will," I said.

We both went quiet, thinking. I still wasn't used to the allied feeling. I'm not much of a team player. I don't have a problem with other people. I like people a lot. I just work better alone. I don't want to have to rely on someone else to get it right, and I don't want someone relying on me when I get it wrong. That's why I never excelled at team sports.

French and Rock's radios crackled simultaneously, making us jump from our thoughts.

"What's the word?" Strawn's voice hissed.

I looked at French. This was the moment of truth. Was he going to uphold our freshly forged friendship or not?

French pushed a thumb to a button and spoke sideways, "One in custody; we got him."

"Any problems?" the voice sparked back.

"Not much."

"Good. Bring him here."

"Copy."

French settled back in his seat, and I started moving. I handed him back his gun, slowly, making sure the safety catch was on.

He took it back, holstering it. "I'm on your side. I just want to find Amy; I can't do it without you."

"Thanks," I said, and I meant it.

"What are we going to do?" he asked.

"Well, we've got two problems between the two of us. Strawn and Lang. The smart money would say we stick together, but I don't think we have time."

He nodded. "The snow is picking up, but they've got some state crews working on clearing the roads from the outside."

"Amy and Patton are as good as dead if Lang or Strawn finds them first," I said.

"So let's split up."

That impressed me. My opinion of Carter French was changing markedly. First impressions are often wrong, for me especially.

"Who's going to do what?" he asked.

We were in a pickle. French knew the lay of the land better than I did, but Strawn was expecting French and Rock to roll up any minute in the patrol car, so French could more easily get the drop on him. We deliberated this back and forth. French was better trained in the use of firearms.

I'm comfortable with guns, in a layman sort of way. A lot of folks barely know where the bullets go. But I think guns are quintessential tools that every law-abiding citizen should own and train with. I strongly support the right to keep and bear arms, but it doesn't mean I relish the thought of using them against people, even as rotten as the villains I was up against. I knew Lang was armed, and Strawn would be too. They wouldn't hesitate to shoot us.

"I think I should take Strawn," French said. "All I need to do is put him in a holding cell, and then I can come back and help you. We'll do it together."

"Okay," I said. "I need to get back and check on Agnes and Mary; they could be in danger."

"Bring them to the station; we'll meet there," French said.

From the floor Rock grunted and cursed. I was surprised and grateful he hadn't learned more from the supposed special weapons and tactics training the doctor had mentioned.

French and I looked at him. He rolled and wriggled and managed to sit up, even with his hands cuffed behind his back, using his massive abdominals. He looked at us, grimacing through bloodstained teeth.

"What's going on?"

French said nothing.

But I had an idea. "Hey, Rock, you got a phone?"

He spat at me, which I took issue with. I slapped him on the ear. He tried to fight, rolling and flopping like a fish. I got him on his front, put one knee at the base of his skull, and found his cell phone in a jacket pocket.

"Thanks, Rock. I need to make a call."

As I was swiping and typing with my fingers, I turned to French, who looked a little less sure of himself now that his domineering partner had regained consciousness.

"Hey, man, you'd better get going. He'll be wondering where you are. Call Rock's phone; I'll have it."

French got up and hustled toward the door. Rock yelled after him, threatening and cursing.

"Shut up," I said, cuffing him on the ear again.

I found Mary's name in the phone's contact list, pushing the little green icon to call. It rang and rang and rang and then went to voicemail. Maybe Mary wasn't too keen to talk to Rock, which was fine by me. I left a message and told Mary it was me and to call as soon as she could.

Rock kept yapping at me, but I ignored him. He had made his bed. I couldn't waste time trying to persuade him again. But I couldn't very well leave him defenseless in a known killer's house. What if Lang came back? He probably wouldn't spare his coworker. Rock and I weren't the likeliest candidates for the bosom-buddies-of-the-year award, but I didn't want to see him dead. I whistled loudly from the door, and French turned back. I motioned for him, and he hurried inside again.

"What is it?" he asked, a little breathless.

"We can't leave Rock here. Lang might come back. Let's put him in your car."

Between the two of us we carried Rock outside. He struggled, making us lose our grips, but after our third time dropping him into the snow, he settled down enough we were able to stuff him into the back seat. Maybe he understood we were trying to protect him. Or maybe he was thinking of how else to curse us.

I clapped French on the shoulder. "Good luck, man. See you soon." He nodded, a determined glint in his eyes, and left.

I ran across the snow back to Mary's Jeep, threw it into gear, and sped off as fast as I dared. The snow was picking up. The drifts on the side of the road lifted in swirls to meet the falling flakes. It looked like it was snowing from both above and below. The yellow centerline was invisible. I navigated very carefully back to Agnes's, especially on the turns, calling Mary again and again.

No answer.

Mary was a smart, conscientious person. Even if she hadn't heard the voicemail, she would have answered after the fourteenth call, maybe exasperatedly or assuming it had to be an emergency. But there was no answer.

I got worried. I was getting into deeper and deeper water. There is a quote by the second-greatest man who ever lived, Joseph Smith: "Perhaps I am meant to swim in deep waters; better deep than shallow." But I was more worried than I'd ever been. I was no Joseph. I would have preferred the shallows.

I neared the turn by the church building. Above the trees I saw smoke.

CHAPTER FOURTEEN

Not a lot of smoke though. Not the black, billowing mass you'd expect from a house fire. This was just the thin, lazy, white tendril from a wood-burning stove, which meant they were still there. I exhaled with relief, bumping down the lumpy road.

I drove beyond Agnes's driveway and backed in. Parking nose out is always smart. It takes just a moment's more time and an ounce more skill to back in, but it can save you if you need to get out in a hurry—a distinct tactical advantage. It's safer, too, in case of pedestrians walking in parking lots and such, not that I expected much foot traffic here, but I backed in anyway.

As I climbed out of the Jeep, I moved Rock's pistol from my pocket to the waistband of my jeans. It felt a little heavy and awkward.

Mary met me at the door with a hug, which was a little unexpected but much appreciated. I can remember being told on a few occasions that I give good hugs, not that I consider it much of a skill. It's not rocket science. It's like a handshake or smiling or breathing. You just do it.

Mary and I held the hug much longer than necessary. Mary's hug seemed to say all kinds of things, like, *I missed you, I was worried about you* or, *Thanks for not crashing my car* or maybe nothing.

"Where's your phone? I've been calling."

She patted her front pockets and then her back ones and stuck her hands into her sweater pouch.

"Must be downstairs. I'm sorry."

Agnes appeared in the entryway as I stamped my boots and shut the door. It was warm and cozy inside. The table was cleared. The sink was empty.

"You missed chow," she said.

"Couldn't be helped," I said. "I'm sorry."

"Want to tell me what's going on?" Agnes asked.

So I told her. I laid out the series of events as I understood them, adding inferences where needed. During the whole explanation she said nothing, only moving to bite her lip or nod almost imperceptibly. She barely even blinked, like she was trying to simultaneously picture the scene in her mind and also block the awful images out.

Agnes started lacing up her winter shoes. "Let's go," she said.

Mary started pulling on a coat, hat, and gloves. "I'll drive."

The roads had been bad since I had gotten there. Now they were worse, much worse. Mary was a competent driver, better than I was, and she had lived here all her life. But she said the forecast had not called for snow like this and that, despite living in rural Montana, she did not have a lot of experience driving through snow. Her theory was, she said, that if it was too snowy to drive normally, then it was too snowy to go out at all.

At turtle speed we managed to clear the unpaved road and pass the church.

I rode shotgun, except I didn't have a shotgun—I had a pistol, which I hoped would be enough. I didn't want to kill anyone, not even Lang, as atrocious as he was. But you have to be prepared. Because bad guys will always have an advantage if they don't have the same inhibitions as you. It was like Captain Moroni said: "I do not delight in the shedding of blood." He was not bloodthirsty, but he defended his people vehemently, even to the shedding of blood. I wasn't bloodthirsty either, which was probably why I had never made it big as a professional fighter, which was fine by me. The fewer people who knew my name, the better. I was not a recluse or a hermit, not entirely dysfunctional or crazy; I just liked my privacy.

Mary navigated her way to the police station. We didn't stop at any of the intersections—couldn't, really—just slid along as if pulled by an invisible string.

We pulled up in front of the station, all of us swiveling our heads back and forth for any signs of life. Or death.

My Buick was there. French's vehicle was there.

I told them both to wait there, just until I had checked it out.

"No way," they said in unison.

I sighed. I couldn't argue with them. "Just stay behind me."

Climbing out, we bunched up and moved toward the double doors, still scanning and searching for danger. Once inside, we stopped. There was no fire in the pit, and night was coming on fast. The station felt like a long-abandoned building, eerily dark and oppressively silent.

We formed a tight triangle, with me at the head. I kept my arms spread out like the wings of an airplane, partly to shield Mary and Agnes from any attack and partly to keep them from wandering ahead of me.

That is when I noticed the blood, plenty of it, but not as much as I would have expected from gunshot wounds and certainly not as much as I had seen on the agent's car seat. There were patches of little round drops in nice, linear trails, and long splattered lines along the walls, shaped like the paisley patterns you see on ties. A forensic scientist could have figured out a lot based on the trajectories of the blood drops.

We moved behind Lang's desk. The door leading to the inner offices was smashed off its hinges. There were two schools of thought when going through a doorway like that. One was to hold it up by the handle and slowly, gently glide it open. The other was to just put it out of its misery. I split the difference, nudging it as far as it would go of its own accord, which wasn't much, and followed that with a tremendous push kick that sent it crashing inward.

Nothing.

Agnes and Mary were as tightly wound as cello strings. I could almost feel their vibrations and tremors next to me. The desks were mostly overturned, and the computer monitors and phones had fallen in tangles of wire. We all turned as one at a sound from behind a desk. It was a burbling, gurgling groan. Mary found a light switch and lit up the overhead fixtures. Peering around, we found French moving a mangled hand through the air, like a slow-motion wave. He was beaten badly; his eyes were swollen shut under a mask of blood. His hands and arms had signs of defensive injuries. I dove down next to him, careful not to touch the raw wounds.

"Hey, man, it's us. We're here. You're gonna be okay, brother."

He mumbled and groaned.

I looked at Mary and Agnes. They were aghast. I don't think they had ever seen such horrific injuries. "Call the doctor," I said.

Mary was already grabbing a console from the floor.

Blood and spittle dribbled out of French's mouth as he managed to say, "Lang."

"Lang did this to you?"

He tried to nod his head but just slumped. After a minute he managed to mouth, "Yes." Mary and Agnes crowded in to help tend to him, which impressed me. People unaccustomed to blood tend to shrink from the sight of it. Mary was saying the doctor was on his way, and Agnes kept asking where Amy was. French was fading in and out.

I straightened at a noise from behind. That is, to a handful of noises. The rustle of clothing, a groan, a stifled cough, crunching and sliding of grit on the floor as a shoe shifted position.

I turned, and there he was, still wearing my coat. Patton, the man who had hit me over the head and stolen my car. The man who had saved Amy. He was in pretty much the same shape as French, beaten to a pulp. His lips were puffy and split over bloodstained teeth. He was clutching his side as though he was afraid it was going to split. Busted ribs, I figured; his breathing was shallow, like he didn't want to stretch them too far. I stood and moved slowly over to him. One leg was partially pinned by a fallen desk. I lifted it off him, and he opened his eyes. They were bleary and filled with surprise and relief.

I squatted down next to him. "Where's Amy?"

He shook his head and moved his hand off his ribs, slowly, holding it up in a placatory sign of contrition.

I felt Agnes move behind me.

Laboriously, Patton said, "I panicked when we crashed. I'm sorry, really. I had to get Amy out, I had laid her in the trunk; I thought it would be safer."

"How did you end up at her house in time to save her?" I asked.

"I was hunting a wolf—you know, the four-legged kind," he said.

"And what about outside Agnes's house?" I asked.

He exhaled through clenched teeth, combating the throbs and shots of pain that must have racked his body. "Amy and I were coming to warn Agnes about Lang, but we saw you there. I knew you and the cops had talked, since I called them anonymously after I knocked you out. I told them where you were. I didn't want you to freeze to death, but I didn't know whose side the cops were on. We came back late that night to Agnes's house to try again, but you were still there and came out after us."

I looked at Agnes; she appeared focused and ready for action, intent on Patton's every word.

"Where is Amy now?" I repeated.

"He's got her," he said, coughing.

Agnes growled. "Come on, Sawyer; let's go get her."

I nodded at her. "You did good, Patton. It couldn't have been easy, doing what you did." I felt a wave of compassion for Patton, even if he had ruined my coat. The sleeves were torn, and the front was bloodstained. "The doctor's on his way. I'll handle Strawn and Lang. I'll find Amy; they can't have gone far."

Patton, who was struggling to stay coherent, looked at me sharply. "No, no. It's just Lang."

CHAPTER FIFTEEN

Just Lang? Then, where did Strawn fit in all of this? My reasoning and deductions and conclusions were eroding. Agnes and Mary were moving and talking behind me. I didn't hear what they said.

From behind a jumble of overturned furniture another figure crawled. It was Strawn, beaten, battered, and whipped worse than French and Patton put together. His eyebrows were cut and bleeding, and his moustache was stained red. But he was stronger than them, too, more awake and alert. He pulled himself to his feet.

Agnes helped Strawn to a chair, and I looked at him. His face was drawn with pain, but his eyes were beseeching.

"What happened here?" I asked. Considering the state of French and Patton, I thought it prudent to get Strawn's version of events too.

"Lang took her; he beat us, all three of us. We never saw him coming. French drew on me; I thought he was in on it somehow. I grabbed him and asked him what was going on. Patton and Amy came through the door, and I couldn't believe it. That's when Lang showed up. Amy ran in here from the lobby, and Lang followed. We all ended up here. None of us could shoot with Amy so close. He laid into us and got away with her."

"Did you kill Arlene?" I said.

His eyes flashed, and he grimaced more, but this time maybe not from physical pain. He shook his head. "No."

I nodded; I believed him. I took the photo of the two of them out of my pocket and let it float down to him.

"You don't have to keep your secret anymore," I said.

"Thank you," he said, his eyes brimming with decades-old tears.

"Where did they go?" I asked Strawn.

"I don't know, but you can do it—you can get my daughter back."

His voice was much the same as when I'd first met him, with the same steady command, the same self-assuredness. Physically he was out of action, but mentally he was all there.

I went out to the lobby just as the doctor came through the front doors, looking professionally concerned but not disturbed. He must have sped. Maybe he had chains on his tires.

I jerked my head behind me. "Through there."

Agnes and Mary had paused for a beat and then followed. Mary touched my elbow with one hand and handed me her keys with the other. I doubt she had seen so much violence in her whole life. She looked scared but resolute. She was a tough girl.

I pulled Rock's pistol from my waistband and handed it to her.

"What am I supposed to do with this?" she asked.

"Nothing, I hope. But if worse comes to worst, you use it. Don't try to aim—just move naturally, like you're pointing your finger."

She looked like she would protest but said nothing. I handed her the spare magazines too.

Agnes moved to follow me, but I held up a hand. "Ma'am, you'll do more good here. Please." I couldn't focus on rescuing Amy if I had more collateral damage just waiting to happen to worry about.

She looked like she had something to say but just swallowed and nodded as if to say, *Be careful.*

She took the gun gently from Mary's hands, ejected the magazine, checked the slide, tested the action, and reloaded. She racked the slide expertly and nodded resolutely to me.

More good here.

I turned and went out the front door. The cold slapped me in the face again. The darkening sky seemed to amplify the icy wind.

I took a minute to pause at my Buick. It was unlocked. I retrieved the one thing I could use as a weapon. As much as I wanted to drive my own car again, I knew Mary's Jeep was better-equipped to handle the snow. I climbed into Mary's Jeep, adjusting the seat and mirror as I drove out into the coming night.

It was slower going than I would have liked. I could sense the lack of traction, and every turn was a challenge to negotiate. There were no other drivers, no pedestrians, and no animal crossings. I ignored the stop signs.

I thought of Lang's house. Maybe now that he was sure he had taken out the bulk of the opposition he would feel safe in visiting his lair.

He didn't know I was on his trail, which was a distinct advantage.

I was going to need a lot of those. He had probably taken Strawn and French's guns and probably had his own, but he seemed to have a sadistic flair for the long, drawn-out, excruciating pain only achieved with one's hands, which was fine with me.

I like to think of myself as a pretty good fighter. What started as playground honor duels had turned into amateur boxing matches and professional cage fights. Of course, I had been out of training for two years. As a missionary I served, ate, slept, and prayed. Walking miles a day had kept me from getting fat, and wrestling now and again with my fellow missionaries had kept me limber, but I was a far cry from where I had been before. In my little scrap with Rock I had been lucky, and Lang looked like a real smooth operator. He had taken on three tough, motivated men and made mincemeat out of them. Three.

I should have kept Rock's gun. It would have saved me a considerable amount of trouble.

From memory I drove until I came to the dead-end street where Lang lived. In the driveway, there was Lang's tricked-out truck. Lights were on in the house.

Foolishly I had forgotten to turn off my headlights. I'd lost the element of surprise. I didn't think I could just go up and knock on the door with the whole missionary routine. I considered just driving through his living room wall, but I didn't want to inadvertently hurt Amy. The one saving grace I expected was for Lang to not recognize me in the Jeep as someone he had to watch out for. It wasn't my Buick, and it wasn't a cop car. Maybe he would hesitate just long enough.

I drove slowly, planning to turn around at the end of the street, but suddenly I saw a wide-eyed shape pressed up against the rear passenger window of the truck.

Bang bang bang. Bang bang bang.

Bullets thudded into the Jeep's body. My window was shot out, and the front left light went dark. Stamping on the gas, I ducked down and spun the wheel. Once I got the Jeep turned around, I flipped the stalk turning my one remaining light to bright. I peered up and saw Lang standing in the road. He fired a few more shots. I stayed low and lurched the Jeep forward, hoping to hit him. The bullets hit but didn't break the windshield—just cratered and spiderwebbed it. Lang was quick and jumped into the driver's seat of his truck. He leaned out his window, firing one-handed. I backed up to get a better angle and avoid the hot lead, but that gave Lang enough clearance to peel out of the driveway, smashing the Jeep's right side. The impact was low-speed, but the truck was big, and it sent me rocking. Lang rammed the truck forward, fishtailing as he made the turn. Gritting my teeth, I peered through the clear spots in the windshield and followed. I wondered if people would call the cops after hearing the gunshots, but this was the middle of Nowhere, Montana. People were probably shooting stuff all the time—street signs, cans, varmints, game, each other—so the shots might not have garnered any suspicion.

Who would they call anyway?

The snow slowed Lang down, but he was still widening the gap between us. He got smart and slowed when I took a turn onto the next spoke to cut the distance. He ended up behind me, and as I stopped to turn around, he got past me. I followed. He was a hundred yards ahead, but by then, my single high beam was fixed on his bumper. He was driving toward the twelve o'clock spoke, out of town.

I remembered French saying crews were working on clearing the roads from the other side. Had they yet?

I fishtailed at one point, and he gained ground. I thought I saw a pale face peering out from the rear window again. At least I knew Amy was still alive, but I couldn't run him off the road for fear of injuring her.

I'm no Hollywood stunt driver, but this was a no-brainer: follow him until he had to stop at the impassable snowbank, if it was still impassable. But I did not want him to get that far, so I just crashed into him. Moving over to the wrong lane, I sped up alongside him. He sped up too. I waited until my nose was level with his tail and then, jerking the wheel to the right, I sent him into a spin. This time I was ready for the collision. It was no accident.

I started to lose control and spin. I wasn't ready for that. I tried to fight it, but the Jeep was top heavy. I hit the road's edge on two tires. The passenger side was angled up to the sky and my side hung over a steep, snowy hill. The Jeep tipped a little more. I hadn't worn my seatbelt, so I clambered up to the passenger door and opened it like the hatch on a submarine. I jumped and rolled out onto the street. The Jeep scraped and slipped and tipped and tumbled down the hill, smashing some trees by the sound of it. I didn't watch it go—just ran toward the police truck.

Amy had somehow gotten out, but Lang was dragging her toward the truck by her legs. His back was toward me, but he turned as I ran. I launched a massive right at Lang's head. He ducked and hit me in the gut. Grunting, I caught him a weak left on the neck as he stepped back.

"Run," I said to Amy, breathlessly.

Lang was grinning wolfishly, flexing his fingers like claws.

"You just cost me my business, boy," he said.

I unzipped my borrowed coat and tossed it aside; it was too restrictive for the kind of fighting I expected, but now the air was too cold. Happily, my adrenaline was already working exactly as nature intended. I didn't need warm fingers or a warm nose to fight.

"I'm about to cost you your freedom," I said.

Lang was a lean guy with a long ropey musculature. He was about as tall as I was but not as broad. I was dismayed to see that, even after fighting Strawn and Patton and French, he didn't have a mark on him.

He was pacing back and forth, eagerly, expectantly, like a predatory zoo animal behind the glass at feeding time. He was dressed in his white winter camouflage. It all looked pretty silly, but I wasn't laughing.

"Who the devil are you, anyway?" he asked.

I should have said something like, *Your worst nightmare* or, *Batman*, but I just said blandly, "Nobody."

"Thought you was Rock at first," he said. "But you're too little."

I ignored that. "Are you going to come quietly?" I asked.

"You planning on taking me all by your lonesome there, *Nobody*?" He sneered.

It was getting dark and cold, and he was strong and fast, and I was distracted by the talking. I hadn't noticed him edging closer until he was in range. He hit me with a right on the edge of my jaw that sent me reeling. Bracing myself against the truck, I pushed off, blocking Lang's left hook with my right forearm. I caught hold of him and spun him around, slamming him against the side of the Ford. He grabbed on to me, and we held on in a death grip. Twisting left and right, we tried to throw each other off-balance, tried to get better leverage. I stomped at his feet, trying to break the little bones in there, but he was nimble. Suddenly he let go with one hand and threw a rabbit punch toward my groin. I twisted, still clinging to Lang, and took the punch on my hip.

The blow stung, and I felt a shock echo numbly through my leg. I got a better hold and threw Lang onto the ground. I didn't give him time to get up. I jumped on top as he tried rolling away. Size matters, no matter what they tell you. Of course, a good fighter can neutralize size or strength advantages, but when it comes to ground fighting, a skilled big guy will beat a skilled smaller guy nine times out of ten.

This must have been the tenth time.

I punched him a couple of times in the face, but as I pulled back to rain some elbows on him, he bucked and rolled and wriggled away. With a lunge I hit him in the face again before we were standing. He got up, lashing out with a kick, and slipped a little, and I caught his foot, pulling him into a split that looked painful. I got up, keeping hold of his foot.

He growled, and I tried to smash his knee joint with a downward elbow. I was too slow. He kicked out with his free foot, knocking me back down.

Lang struck out and cut my lip with a left jab. As he waded in, I punched his lead leg in the thigh. He stumbled back as I regained my footing. He was looking at me with a little more interest. I tried to grab hold of him again, but he flitted backward. I followed. He feinted once, twice. I didn't take the bait. We each led with a right hook. Both strikes connected, rattling each other's teeth.

I dodged a follow-up overhand left and tagged him with a left and a right. He rocked back on his heels, and I leapt in.

But it was a trick. My punches hadn't hurt him. I clinched with him, wrapping his arms, and he slugged away at my ribs. I was taller, so I employed a dirty boxing trick. I came up on my toes and hit him in the chin with my shoulder. We struggled, and he grabbed a handful of my hair with his right, jerking my head back, which was a good move, but it's more effective if you grab someone from behind or if you've got longer arms. Lang didn't.

But I was worried about him attacking my newly exposed throat. Ignoring the pain in my head, I stuck out my own right arm, pushing his face away, keeping him at bay. His incoming left bounced off my shoulder. Snaking my left arm around his right, I isolated the elbow and jerked up, trying to dislocate it.

Grunting, he hopped around, releasing his grip on my hair and trying to relieve the pressure. Then he kicked out, trying to break my knee. I moved just in time to save the joint, ligaments, and cartilage, but the kick caught me on the calf. It hurt, and I went down to one knee. He kicked me again, this time in the ribs, and I hit the ground on my back. He pounced, diving with his knees into my gut.

All the breath fled my lungs, and I gasped for air. He punched me in the sternum. It felt like a sledgehammer cracking through me, breaking the earth's crust and bursting out on the other side of the planet, somewhere in China.

I stabbed upward with my thumbs, toward his eyes, but he arched back, turning away. I hooked my hand around the back of his head, pulling him close enough to get the leverage to roll over. We tumbled in the snow until I got on top.

He didn't have enough hair to grab, so I clamped my hands on either side of his face and smashed his head against the ground. Once, twice, three times. In the summer it would have knocked him unconscious. Or killed him. But in the deep snow it did nothing but cool the back of his head. He turned his head to bite at my hands, and I pulled back as if from a hot stove. He got out from underneath me and kicked me in the face. I fell back, blood spewing from my smashed lips. I still had all my teeth though.

For now.

We got back to our feet and breathed. My chest hurt; each breath felt like a stab.

We moved, circling in a weird interpretive dance to no music other than the blood pounding in our ears. He was smiling through his own bloodied teeth.

I wasn't.

His plans were shot, and he was improvising like a cornered animal—not smart but shrewd, dangerous, and abnormally strong.

Midway through our circling dance, he broke off and ran for the embankment where the Jeep had gone down. He leapt down among the trees, and I followed, stumbling through the snow.

I lost him.

I looked and listened, straining my eyes and ears for a trace. Nothing.

Camouflage.

Then I was hit from behind with the wrecking ball of Lang's shoulder. His charge sent me sprawling face-first into the fresh powder, in a reverse snow angel. If I stayed down, I was dead. I'd become a *real* angel. Maybe.

I pushed up and flopped to the side just as Lang landed with both feet right where my head had been. I got back up just as he got set again.

I hit him in the side of the head with my right elbow, and he knocked the wind out of me again with a body shot. We both caught each other by the collar and simultaneously head-butted one another.

I saw stars. He must have, too, because he let go. I stepped back and nearly fell but caught myself on a tree trunk.

I lost sight of him again. I hoped Amy would just drive away. Now was her chance.

Then I heard Lang. "*Nobody*, was it? What kind of bone you got to pick with me anyway?"

I moved behind the tree trunk, breathing hard and hurting.

"You're a piece of garbage, Lang. I saw your videos."

There was a barking, coyote laugh. "You like those, boy? See that redhead you fancy? Maybe I'll take her along with me and ole Amy."

I said nothing.

I couldn't place him by the direction his voice came from. It sounded so loud in the stillness.

I hadn't even realized the snow had stopped.

He spoke again. "Tell me, *Nobody*, you ready to die for nothing?"

I thought of Mary. Absurdly I imagined wandering through the woods in summertime with her, hand in hand, and stopping beneath a big tree to laugh and talk and kiss.

"I'm right here, Lang," I called back.

"All in good time, *Nobody*, all in good time."

"You killed those federal agents; you won't get away with it."

I heard movement farther up the hill, close to the road. I moved, trying to catch sight of Lang.

"Those feds came to tell little sweet-cheeks all about how her dead momma wasn't murdered after all. After waking up from Patton's cheap shot, I made a plan, and I burned that place down. Figured they would all think those bones were hers and stop looking. Didn't fool you, huh?"

I moved behind another tree, higher up the hill.

"You did, until the doctor told me the bones weren't female and I saw the videos. What happened before?" I asked. Because I had to know.

He came around a tree just as I was moving to it. I threw a jab that he ducked. He tried to tackle me by diving and grabbing at my waist, but I lifted and heaved and swung him around. He landed hard and scrambled back up the slope. I gave chase.

We both got back to the road at the same time. His right fist glanced off my ear and set it ringing. I dealt him a jab that turned into a scything elbow. He backed up and breathed. I waited, needing to catch my own breath.

"It was the perfect crime. Strawn didn't know the feds were coming. I got their call. I handled it. I was free and clear until they found my cameras. The perfect crime, almost."

"No such thing," I said.

He started to say something else but stopped himself. He straightened up, looking wistfully up at the sky. He sighed, letting his hands hang loosely.

"I never wanted to kill anyone, boy. That fool Patton was a friend of mine. I've known Strawn well for years, and I trained French on the job . . ."

He trailed off. I said nothing.

"You're a believer, right? Strawn said you were a preacher of some sort. Do you think there's hope for me?"

He seemed so contrite. I was taken aback. The missionary in me shouted, *Testify!*

"Yes, of course. There's hope for every—"

Then he lunged. He'd tricked me.

I swatted his incoming jab aside but took a follow-up cross to the brow. He tried a knee to my groin, but I got ahold of his leg and jerked up fast. He went down, and I followed.

Odysseus is called the man of twists and turns, and most people think that has to do with his circuitous route home in Homer's *Odyssey*. But there is great significance. Odysseus was crafty and cunning, and he was also a fantastic wrestler, which is all about twisting and turning.

As we grappled I got behind Lang. Wrapping my arms around his waist, I lifted and slammed him down. He tried to roll into me, but I got around to his back again, trying to get a forearm across his throat to choke him into submission. He did all the right things to defend his airway. He tucked his chin and grabbed my forearm with both hands like he was doing a chin-up on the bar at the gym. With my free hand on his forehead I tried to tilt his head back.

He bit at me again, I loosened my grip, and he squirmed away. I was still on the ground, and he turned around, looming over me. He bent to hit me, and I kicked his legs out from under him. As he fell I scrambled up, leaping headlong at him, ready to finish it.

But he must have been counting on that, because he did exactly the right thing. He stuck both feet up in the air so that when I came down his feet were against my midriff. He bent his knees like the leg-press machine in the gym and gave a tremendous push, catapulting me back down the hill.

The downgrade was not especially steep, but my airborne trajectory made it like falling twenty feet. I collided with a tree against my midriff, which halted my flight with the pain of hard bark against soft flesh. I fell and rolled as I landed, end over end, until I came to rest on my back in deep, soft powder.

I wanted to just fall asleep right then and there. I was cold, but the snow felt cozy. It took the edge off my headache and eased the bruising on my knuckles and face and ribs.

But I had to get up. Mind over body, they say. But sometimes it's body over mind. Both mind and body were taxed. Totaled, really. But I still had some fight in me, and beyond body, beyond mind, was spirit.

Regaining my feet, I looked back up the hill. Lang hadn't wasted time. He had gotten a rifle from his truck, maybe the same one he used to shoot all those herbivores he caught unawares. He couldn't miss; I was less than a hundred yards away from him. He was aiming downhill, and there was no wind. I wouldn't make as good a trophy as a four-point buck. I wondered if any of Lang's prey had felt what I felt: completely helpless. Frozen. Like deer in the headlights or rather like a deer in the gunsights.

Then something happened.

There was a blur of movement behind Lang, and he was thrown off balance just as the rifle boomed. The bullet barked a tree next to me.

Amy.

Why hadn't she just run? Not that I minded. She was going after Lang with everything she had.

Lang lost his grip on the rifle, dropping it down the hill. It disappeared into the snow.

Amy had gotten the drop on him, but he was too powerful for her. He seemed to forget all about me as he rounded on her, deflecting her onslaught. Amy, the apparent object of all of his lust, was now the focus of all of his wrath. They moved back away from the edge.

I heard a scream and the meaty crack of a slap.

Not twenty yards from me was Mary's smashed and lifeless Jeep. I hurried to the side of it, reaching through a smashed rear window. I needed something else up my sleeve. I didn't feel any compunction—Lang had resorted to weapons first, which I guess should have flattered me if he didn't think he could keep going barehanded. My shaking hands wrapped around the axe. It was no deer rifle, but the ancient Vikings had done all right for themselves.

I was very glad I had retrieved it from my car before leaving the station. I used it as a walking stick, but I didn't walk—I ran, scrambling back up, up, up the hill to the road and digging into the snow with the haft like it was an extra appendage. I was breathing hard. When I got to the top of the hill Lang's back was to me, which made everything after that much easier. He held Amy by her throat against the rear bumper of the truck. She struggled, and he let go with one hand to slap her again, front hand, back hand.

I have used axes for their intended purpose my whole life. I had gotten some extra practice in lately, what with chopping wood for Agnes, but I had never employed any such implement for such a noble task as I did then.

George Washington's one hundred and ninth rule says, *Let your recreations be manful not sinful.*

Few things are manlier than splitting wood. But Lang was no fabled cherry tree, and I was no Washington.

As Lang's hand pulled back for another slap, I pulled back with the axe like I was preparing for a tennis serve. The two arcs of motion moved more or less in sync, his slap on a more horizontal plane, my downward swing on the vertical.

I like physics a lot, even though I'm no math magician. Force equals mass times acceleration. The axe's head probably weighed two pounds, and I didn't know how fast I was swinging it. Fast enough, apparently, because I beat Lang's slap by a second. My swing was a downward diagonal from right to left.

What would Jesus do?

Fight or flight? Right or wrong? The ultimate binary choices. Despite my urging to run, Amy had chosen to stay and help me. She had saved my life.

She'd chosen to fight. And I chose the right.

Mid-swing I turned the axe so the blunt end kissed the back of Lang's head. He wasn't big enough to crash down like a fallen tree; he just sort of melted straight down, like a witch splashed with water. He released Amy, who slumped down as well. I dropped the axe and caught her. I hoisted her up in my arms. Stepping over Lang's motionless mass, I got Amy into the still-running truck and buckled her in, making sure the heat was on full blast.

Stumbling around like I was on board a fishing boat in rough seas, I found the borrowed coat and put it back on.

I checked on Lang to make sure the blow hadn't killed him. Blunt-force trauma can kill just as well as anything. But he was alive.

You're not getting off that easily, I thought. *You have crimes you've got to answer for.*

CHAPTER SIXTEEN

THE DRIVE BACK TO TOWN was hard. My vision was swimming, and my brain was foggy.

Amy's breathing was steady next to me.

I stayed mostly on the road all the way back. After what seemed forever, I pulled onto the walk in front of the station.

I carried Amy inside; my arms were leaden, and my legs were shaky, but she was as light as any snowflake. Once through the entry I took a couple more wavering paces before sinking to my knees. I tried to call out, but my voice was muted. There was a roaring in my ears like oceans, and I fought the blackness encroaching on the corners of my vision. I kept hold of Amy, swaying like a windsock in a storm.

The inner door opened, and I caught a glimpse of the doctor tending his patients.

Mary and Agnes came through the doorway together. They gave little cries of panicked relief, pain-filled sounds—the audible version of the feeling you get when you pull out a particularly bad splinter or fix a dislocated joint. Pain, pain, pain, followed by gasping, surprised relief.

The doctor came out and helped.

"Another patient for you," I said.

"You or her?"

"I'm fine. Right as rain," I said. Then I sank to the floor and was out like a light.

It didn't last long though. Mary must have thought I had died, because she started shaking me and trying to roll me over

onto my back. I waited for her to try mouth-to-mouth. Didn't
happen. So I got up, brushing myself off.

She was asking me what happened.

"Oh, nothing much," I said, "but I'll be all right."

I staggered back out into the night. Walking to the front of
the truck, I found my less-than-precious cargo. I had lashed Lang
to the hood, just like he might have done to those deer he had
hunted.

He was strapped down tightly. I hadn't wanted him to fall off
and get run over. He was hot under the collar and cold everywhere
else. I dragged him inside and stuffed him into a cell.

* * *

The FBI showed up at first light. The bureau was in full force, with
helicopters and sunglasses and blue jackets with yellow letters.
They had lost two good men and were not taking it lightly. There
were black cars with antennae swarming all over the place. There
was no room at the inn. The owner might have started charging
the summer fare. The Oak Table had a lot of new customers
as well.

The FBI took custody of Lang and raided his house, seizing
his equipment. They taped it off like the crime scene it was.
Rock and French and I had to explain our little tussle, which
was deemed inconsequential by the investigators. They didn't care
about anything but nailing Lang to the wall. I didn't envy him at
all. He would not fare well in prison.

Eventually they revealed what the two murdered agents had
intended on showing Amy. We got to look over the files as the
assistant special agent in charge debriefed us.

The documents were in chronological order. The first chunk
of pages were smudgy photocopies of the twenty-five-year-old
originals. It was Arlene Kirk's dossier. I skimmed over the initial
reports. She had been found on the side of the road, like I had read
online. All signs had indicated an attack. The papers outlined the
rescue efforts, the delivery of the baby, and then Arlene's expiration.

The case had gone cold and had been tucked away into the
bottomless pit of unsolved murders.

Then came the new report. Several trail cameras had been recovered from the area. I hadn't known that there were trail cameras that old. Evidently the guy who had placed the cameras to photograph deer and cougars and bears had passed away, and the cameras had waited silently until some enterprising hikers had gone off the trail and found the mossy machines. They had presented their findings to Park Services. The photographs were not pleasant. Arlene could be seen in several. In one she was walking with a stick, in another she was leaning over in an exaggerated stretch, and then she was on the ground, rolling, falling. The cameras had caught only fragments of the fall, shutters snapping only every half-second or so.

The photos matched the doctor's assessment that it had not been a strong man who had attacked Arlene. There had not been a man at all. The fall over rocks and through brambles explained the inconsistent yet ultimately fatal injuries.

The reports were thorough, if a little long-winded. The slow-moving but unstoppable hybrid of bureaucracy and police work had fired up and begun chugging. There were jurisdictional issues. Back in the day it had all been handled by county police. With the latest news, the park rangers were involved, and the Seattle police came on board since she had been a resident at the time of her death. A couple of county guys were still around and chipped in what they could remember.

What had been thought to be a murder had been an accident. No details had been provided to the press, the report said, pending notification of next of kin. Eventually the FBI had tracked down the rest of the Kirk family in Cluff. They'd assigned the easy job to two seasoned agents who had just come off a big case. The agents had contacted local law enforcement; a Sergeant Lang was cited. Like he had told me, he had been the one to take the call, and as a sergeant, he took charge. It had all unraveled for Lang when the agent had noticed the hidden camera at Amy's house. Lang had panicked and improvised. His own video convicted him.

So that was it, simple as that.

Lang had killed the men sent to bring closure to the victim's daughter and sister. He had started the fight, and we had ended it.

* * *

The next few days were all about convalescence. The doctor had a nice setup in his home for Strawn, French, and Patton. It was not like in the movies. You don't recover from a bad beating right away. I was still on the mend myself. Those same few days saw me going through an inventory every morning, like a pilot doing a preflight check, ascertaining the fullness and mobility of every limb and muscle. There were strained muscles for sure, and my ribs didn't feel quite right. Breathing deeply was painful. I had plenty of ugly bruises and scrapes and some cuts on the inside of my mouth, and my knuckles were not pretty. No breaks though. No fractures or sprains. Nothing permanent. My cognitive functions seemed normal. The human body is a mostly self-healing machine. It just takes time.

On the third day, I brought food from the café to the doctor's house. Strawn was watching sports by himself. He asked me to turn the TV off. Though he was diminished somewhat, he still had his command presence. He must have been relieved of a big, twenty-five-year-old, tragic weight. It must have torn him up to be so close to his daughter all those years and unable to bridge the gap because of fear of reprisal for a crime he hadn't committed.

He'd been away working, and on that fateful day Arlene had gone for a hike, despite being so far along in her pregnancy. In hindsight Strawn said he might have had a solid alibi, but in the moment, he had panicked at the thought of investigations, trials, possible imprisonment, and not seeing his child. After his initial flight, it had been all the more difficult to come forward as the father.

"Sawyer," he said.

"Yes?"

"I want to thank you. You went above and beyond the call of duty."

"You're welcome, sir."

Most people say, *It was nothing* or, *No problem*, which aren't good responses, because they're untrue. This had been a big problem. It had been something.

So I just stuck with tried and true *You're welcome.*

I moved to leave the room, but Strawn stopped me. "Sawyer?"

"Yes, sir?"

"How many chances do you get to raise a daughter?"

That was a heck of a question, one I had limited knowledge about. I had sisters, but that didn't count. I didn't have any kids, didn't have a degree in children's health and development.

Strawn's eyes were deep, filled with worry that he was about to snatch defeat from the jaws of victory. He had been reunited with his girl, only to face the possible reality that she was too far gone, that they would never be father and daughter.

"Chief," I said. "I believe families can be together forever. And forever is plenty of time to make up for lost time. In answer to your question, how many chances do you get, I guess as many as she'll give you."

He nodded, slowly.

I continued. "And she is as resilient as they come. She's tough like you. I wouldn't have made it if she hadn't fought Lang herself. I told her to run, but she stayed."

Strawn smiled.

I gave my regards to Patton, French, and the doctor, saw myself out, and went to enjoy the bright, clean mountain air.

CHAPTER SEVENTEEN

ON THE MORNING OF THE last day I ever spent in Cluff, I walked into the Oak Table Café to a scene of merry chaos.

Everyone was chattering about the happy turn of weather and the resolution of the big case.

I hadn't seen Rock since I had laid him out. He was leaving the café as I entered. He held a Styrofoam container. He paused, and I paused. Finally I stuck my hand out.

"I'm sorry. No hard feelings?"

He looked from my face to my hand. Then he shook it with a little bit of a crushing force in the fingers. He turned to leave. In the aftermath of all that had happened, I had forgotten to give Rock his phone back, and he hadn't asked for it. Maybe he didn't use it much. Or maybe he was too proud to ask me for anything, even his own property. I felt the thin rectangle in my pocket and pulled it out. It had a case of some composite material named for a marine mammal. It had fared better in the fight than I had. I should have use the phone as a weapon. It seemed indestructible.

"Rock," I said.

He turned back toward me, and I tossed the phone to him underhand. He caught it deftly, gave what might have been a tight-lipped smile, and nodded to me. Then he was gone.

Patton was in a back booth. There was a dark-haired woman across from him, maybe a girlfriend. Strawn, French, and Amy were all nearby, not talking much but smiling contentedly. Max the dog lay on the floor nearby.

I ignored the sign on the brass pole and seated myself.

Everyone nodded at me.

I sat alone.

I saw Mary duck periodically in and out of the kitchen, handling trays laden with dishes. I tried to catch her eye, but she seemed pretty busy.

After I had eaten, paid, and was enjoying another cup of cocoa, Mary came and sat opposite me. She looked great. Her hair was done in such a way that it looked undone but functional, pulled back out of her face and spilling down on her shoulders like a brilliant, fiery cascade. Her apple cheeks were flushed with work and the heat of the kitchens. She wore no makeup, which was refreshing to see. She smiled but looked hesitant, like she had something she needed to ask but didn't want the answer to.

I set my mug down.

She looked me in the eye. "Why didn't you kiss me that first night we spent together?"

"As a general rule I don't kiss on the first date," I said.

"Is that what we're doing now? Dating?"

"Is that what you want?" I asked.

"I don't know. I mean, I like you. I mean, I like the *idea* of you. You are so sweet and cheerful and kind and just plain good. I liked seeing you help people, and I just felt safe with you. You're different."

"Thanks," I said.

"How do you feel?"

"A lot better. Real good after all that praise," I said.

"No, I mean about everything."

"I don't feel anything about it. It's just one of those things. Good, if anything. Great, I guess. Happy. Satisfied."

"No post-traumatic stress?" she asked.

"Nope, and no seasonal disorder either."

She smiled. "So what are you going to do now?"

I picked my mug up again and looked inside. Just dregs. Outside I saw the semitruck from the motel roll up and park on the far side of the road. The driver got out and started toward the café. He was smartly dressed in a shirt and tie, sports coat, and slacks. A well-dressed truck driver. It seemed a little absurd. It made me smile.

"You could stay. I'm sure Strawn would hire you; he has to replace Lang. Or Agnes—you'd get good tips working here. You could pay me back for totaling my Jeep," Mary said.

I looked over at the well-dressed truck driver waiting to be seated. Mary stood up.

"Well, let's consider this a *second* date." She moved toward me, bent, and kissed my cheek. It was quick and shy and altogether chaste.

She straightened up. "I've got to get back to work."

She disappeared into the kitchen.

I dug in my pocket and came out with my car key and the receipt from the auto shop in town. The lady there had looked over the Skylark with an eagle eye before telling me that of course she could fix it but that it would be a couple of weeks before it was road-worthy again. She said it would be a pleasure to work on and that besides the recent damage, the Buick was mint. I had paid upfront for the parts and the estimated labor, plus a little more for extras. I left the receipt and key on the table.

Agnes came by.

"You were right; it looks like things really do tend to work out," she said, glancing at Amy and French and Strawn. "More cocoa?"

"No, thanks. But will you give these to Mary for me, please?"

She tilted her head and said, "Sawyer, I'm going to miss you." She pocketed the key and receipt in her apron. "What am I supposed to tell her to do with the car?"

I shrugged. "Whatever she wants. Keep it, sell it, but for Pete's sake, don't crash it."

I stood up, and we hugged. Someone called to her for a refill, and Agnes stepped away.

As I walked toward the door, the truck driver was leaving, too, carrying his meal to go.

He smiled at me, and I asked him, "Are you headed south?"

He nodded and agreed to give me a ride. He said he would be ready in an hour and to meet him back by his rig.

I took a long walk to the store, keeping track of the time in my head. I needed new clothes, and I figured I could just junk my soiled ones.

There was a greasy-haired guy at the counter who nodded to me as I pushed through the doors. There were all sorts of things I had no use for, but in the back corner I found clothing racks. I picked out an olive-colored long-sleeve shirt with three buttons at the top. It was soft at a subatomic level—some sort of new cotton blend. It was as much as a meal for two at the Oak Table. I found some heavy work pants in a dark tan, also too expensive, but I didn't have much choice. I found a plaid button-up that was mostly green with other colors mixed in. Another couple of meals' worth.

I kept my boots because there was nothing better in the store than the ones I had. Then I found a coat rack. Patton had emphatically apologized because my coat had been torn and stained in his fight with Lang.

All of the store's coats were more than a hundred dollars. In disbelief I shook my head and put the coats back. I figured it would be more cost effective to just head south, somewhere where I didn't need one. I settled on a gray wool watch cap for the interim. I also added a pair of white socks.

I changed into the new duds in a dressing room, tearing off the tags as I went and transferring my pocket junk. Walking out, the clerk looked at me strangely. I laid the tags on the counter. He paused for a beat and then rang them up. I paid him and asked for a trash can. Without a word he held up a bin from under the counter. I tossed my old clothes in but kept the borrowed coat.

The guy seemed to remember how to speak, and he asked me if I wanted a receipt.

"No, thank you," I said, turning to leave.

"Cup of cocoa?"

I turned back. The guy was filling a Styrofoam cup from an insulated apparatus on the counter next to the register.

"Sure, thanks," I said.

"We have cocoa in the winter. We do iced tea or lemonade in the summer."

I felt better in clean clothes, and as I hustled back to the Oak Table, I tried the cocoa. It was lukewarm sugary mud. I spat out the mouthful and dumped the rest of the mess into a snowbank.

That was it, the end of an era. The upward trend of the cocoa scale had bubbled and burst. Time to move on.

Inside the café the well-dressed truck driver had finished his meal and had taken a second order to go. I trashed the empty cup.

I took the coat I had borrowed and draped it over the brass pole that asked me to please wait to be seated.

Climbing up into the semi, I found the inside to be neat and spacious. The driver fired it up, and we sat in silence for a ways, both seeming to enjoy the company and appreciate the quiet.

I felt in my pocket and took out Mary's photograph. I looked at it for a long, sweet minute, committing to memory our conversations, the sound of her voice, the smile lines at the corners of her eyes, her rosy cheeks. Full lips. The long red hair. Her fire and zest and all the feelings I felt when we were near. All the things you can easily forget. Things I hoped to never forget. I bundled those memories up, sealed the envelope, and filed it away under the ever-growing section of *Good* in the unlimited library of my mind.

I had told her I had met people on my mission who had meant so much to me in the moment but then it was on to the next moment. I hoped it would be the same for her, that she would go on to the next moment.

I looked out from my perch in the passenger seat of the semi, high above the pavement that melted away behind us like the wake of a ship. Looking up, I could see the sky, and it was long and clear and blue.

ABOUT THE AUTHOR

BRETT CAIN WAS BORN JUST outside of Chicago and moved at thirteen to the small town of Sequim, Washington. He won a silver medal for boxing and competed in mixed martial arts. After serving as a missionary in Peru, Brett attended Southern Virginia University, where he founded the Ironclad Martial Arts club and studied Spanish and creative writing, which he continued to study during a summer semester at Brigham Young University. He has lived a lot of what he writes and even skipped his finals to aide in the search of a missing little girl. Brett changed his focus from ultimate fighting to writing when he started a family and is working to become a police officer. He lives in Olympia, Washington, with his wife, Madelynne, and their daughter, Josephine.

Enjoy this sneak peek of
Traci Hunter Abramson's novel, coming March 2019,

SANCTUARY

CHAPTER 1

ACE STOOD AT THE HELM of the cabin cruiser and turned away from the cluster of water traffic near the harbor. He couldn't believe he was doing this. He couldn't believe he was here.

His last trip to Maine had come only weeks before his death. It had been fall then too. One unexpected incident, one pivotal decision, had changed his life. Or, rather, had ended it. He had been only twenty years old.

As a guardian, he and the others like him had all made the same decision: in order to live, they had chosen to die.

The wind on his face today assured him his death had been a facade, a ruse to make sure the men who wanted him dead didn't have cause to succeed. Now, only weeks after his fortieth birthday, he found himself looking back and wondering what life would have been like had he been given the opportunity to live a normal life.

Turning inland, he navigated between a series of private islands before making his way toward shore. He saw a small harbor in the distance and checked his coordinates to confirm he was in the right place.

The small village of Eastcrest stretched a couple blocks inland and centered around the main street that led straight to the water. A scattering of clapboard houses dotted the surrounding countryside. Ace doubted the town's population exceeded a thousand.

At the dock, a handful of sailboats bobbed in the water, along with recreational speedboats. More than half the slips were empty, and Ace suspected those belonged to the fishing vessels that were still out on the water this time of day. Either that or tourists who had already gone south for the winter.

He glanced skyward and judged the time to be only ten in the morning. He supposed he needed to invest in another watch, but his cell phone kept the time well enough that he hadn't bothered to replace the watch that had broken a few weeks earlier.

He turned toward the far side of the harbor, where a fuel station was situated on a long dock. As he motored forward, he adjusted his sunglasses and tugged his cap a little lower. No need to give anyone the ability to recognize him.

A man in his sixties approached when he pulled up to the dock.

Ace nodded a greeting before he tossed him a line, and the two men secured the boat.

"I need to top off, and I hoped you could direct me to the harbor master. I need a place to dock for a couple days."

"You're looking at him." Methodically, the older man went about refueling the boat. "You can take slip twenty-two. It's been open since old man Watkins passed away last summer."

"Thanks." Ace looked over the small harbor again, taking note of the way the man had referred to the previous owner of his temporary docking space. He was tempted to ask if he knew the location of the woman Ace had been sent here to find, but that sort of question would bring far too much unwanted attention. His presence alone was likely to circle through town by noon.

A few minutes later, he secured his boat once more and took a look at the village of Eastcrest. The size gave him hope that his search would be short-lived, but just the thought of succeeding sent a wave of apprehension through him.

Kristi Hartinger. Her name had been one of more than a hundred the guardians had considered for this job, but no matter how many other possibilities he'd offered, she remained firmly at the top of everyone's list.

The real question wasn't if she would accept the position he was here to offer her but, rather, if she would forgive him for letting her think he'd been dead for the past twenty years.

* * *

Kristi leaned on the railing of the wide deck, a cup of hot chocolate cradled in her hands. She took a sip, enjoying the warmth that seeped through her in contrast to the cold snap in the air. On the cliffs below, water crashed against rock and sent a spray into the air that smelled of the sea.

Across the span of water between her home and the mainland, the early-morning light shimmered on the ocean and lit the blooming colors of fall along the shore. She loved this time of year in Maine. If only she had more time to enjoy it.

She wandered to the other end of the porch and checked the cove where her boat swayed gently in the water beside the wooden dock. Sunlight glimmered on the foam of the waves as the water rolled onto the sandy beach that stretched beyond the inlet. The guesthouse on the bluff overlooking the beach stood empty, a reminder that tourist season was coming to a close.

Taking the last sip of her hot chocolate, she headed inside. Time to get this day started.

As though reading her thoughts, Samson, the black Labrador Retriever lying on the deck, wagged his tail.

"Come on, you."

Expecting the dog to comply, she went inside and put her mug in the kitchen sink. She glanced toward the hallway leading to her office but chose not to think about the work piled on her desk.

On days like today, she wished she could simply live off her land as her ancestors once had, but in truth, she knew she needed the mental stimulation her day job provided. Creating financial analyses for an online investing site might not be as interesting as managing a multibillion-dollar mutual fund or overseeing the finances of military security forces overseas, but it was something.

She had done both of the other jobs during the ten years she had lived away from her home state of Maine, but a bad breakup, an overbearing boss, and the death of her grandfather had ultimately pushed her to change her life drastically and settle here on Heritage Island, the private island that had been in her family for two centuries. The hundred twenty acres that spanned the area behind her house were still largely untouched. Nearly a hundred acres were virgin forest, with another twenty of apple trees. Blueberry and cranberry bushes flanked the orchard on one side and ensured that she had an ample supply of fruit to last her the year and still have plenty to sell or share.

Her stomach knotted at the thought that her life here could be coming to an end. She shook her head, pushing away the possibility and the stress that always came with it. "Enjoy today," she said to herself.

She walked onto her front porch, her gaze drawn to where two deer grazed on the lawn. They lifted their heads and studied her for a brief moment as though sizing up a potential threat.

"Just stay out of my flowerbed," Kristi warned. The past two summers, she had planted dozens of flowers, and so far, none of them had survived the deer's appetites.

Clearly not concerned with her presence, they both lowered their heads and continued to nibble the grass. When Samson raced down the stairs, though, the deer reconsidered the location of their morning meal and bounded across the yard and into the trees.

"Come on, boy." She nodded at her dog as she picked up a bucket off the porch, then started toward the ducks' nesting area. "Let's go find some eggs for breakfast."

* * *

"I'm tired of waiting." Dusty hands slammed down on the polished cherry desk.

One eyebrow lifted. "Another couple months and this will all be over."

"Another couple months that we can't start construction," he countered. "If we wait until the court date in November, it will be too late to get the materials onto the island. We'll lose an entire season."

"My hands are tied. What do you suggest I do?"

"Seems to me that if Kristi Hartinger decided to drop the lawsuit, things would go much more smoothly."

"You've already offered to buy her out at three times the assessed value." The annoyance that money hadn't solved the problem surfaced. "She wasn't interested. Remember?"

"I think she's getting a little too comfortable out there by herself." He tilted his head to one side. "If things were a bit tougher, she might reconsider."

The implications hung in the air.

"I'll have to see what we can do."

"You tell me when, and I'll be happy to lend my services."

"Good to know."

CHAPTER 2

TWO DAYS AND NOTHING. WHERE was Kristi? And how was Ace supposed to locate her when all he had was a post office box number? On his first day, he had planted a surveillance camera outside the post office to make sure he didn't miss her when she came to town. Since that time, he had spent countless hours in the town offices and the library digging through old phone books and land records. So far, he hadn't found the golden nugget that told him where she was living.

She wasn't listed as a property owner, nor could he find any record of her parents or grandparents paying local property taxes. All of his information had led him to believe she had moved here after inheriting her family's land, but she had never mentioned anything about the location of that land beyond the name of the town.

He thought of the year they had spent together in high school, he a senior and she a sophomore. They had started out as acquaintances, and within weeks, she had become one of his closest friends. By the time he graduated, that friendship had turned into more, and he had once thought she was the woman he would someday marry. A visit home during his sophomore year of college had smashed those dreams and left a tombstone in the local cemetery with his name on it. He had never seen Kristi again.

Possible scenarios played through his mind over and over about how she would react when she saw him again. He couldn't begin to imagine the betrayal she would feel when she learned the truth. Would she be able to forgive him? Would she even listen to the proposal the guardians wanted to offer her?

In an attempt to stay below the radar, Ace had chosen to camp on his boat as he watched and waited for Kristi. She hadn't shown up at the post office to retrieve her mail, and the surveillance device he had planted near her box established that no one else had come to collect it for her.

His cell phone rang, the shrill sound startling a handful of seagulls perched on the pilings. "Hello?"

"Ghost, it's Jim Whitmore."

"Hello, Senator. What can I do for you?"

"I wanted to check in and see if you've had any luck."

"Nothing yet."

"We only have two weeks. Funding will come through on October 3."

"It's only been two days." He briefly debated the consequences of what would happen if he couldn't find Kristi or, worse, if she refused the job he was here to offer. "Do you have a backup plan if this doesn't work out?"

"You know as well as I do that she was head and shoulders above everyone else we considered," Jim said. "Like you said, it's only been two days."

Two days of sitting on edge, imagining one scenario after another of what Kristi would do, what she would say when she discovered the truth. "I'll give you a call when anything changes."

"Good luck."

"Thanks." Ace hung up and checked his surveillance feed again. Still nothing.

Moving topside, he stood on the deck and stared out at the water, the midday sun reflecting off the waves. Kristi had to be here somewhere.

He pondered the irony for a moment. For twenty years, Ace had lived in the shadows, unknown to the world. Now he was searching for the woman he had left behind, and she was proving to be every bit as invisible as he was.

A sailboat turned toward the harbor, slowing as it approached. Ace looked up, his gaze shifting to the woman at the helm.

Instantly, his breath caught. "Kristi." The single word escaped in a whisper and caught on the breeze.

The curve of her neck, her comfortable stance at the helm took him back in time. How many times had they gone out on the water together?

The brown hair that fed through the back of her ball cap was longer than he remembered, but her appearance hadn't changed much despite the lifetime that had separated them.

She motored into a slip a dozen spaces away. Ace lowered his head, using his own hat to shield his face in case she glanced his way. He needn't have bothered. The moment she reached the dock, she secured her boat and stepped ashore, her focus on the road leading into town.

* * *

The wind whipped at her ponytail as Kristi headed into the village. She waved at Wally Brown, the harbor master, as she passed by the fueling station and started up the hill. Cars lined Main Street in front of the various businesses, but the pedestrian traffic had dwindled significantly over the past two weeks.

She reached her first stop and passed through the door of the post office. "Hey, Bill."

"Kristi. I haven't seen you in a few days. How's everything?"

"Not bad." She retrieved a stack of envelopes from her purse. "Samson's thinking about keeping the deer out of my garden."

"You know, I'm happy to come take care of a few for you."

"Once hunting season opens, I might take you up on that." Kristi handed him her outgoing mail and leaned against the counter. "Especially if you convince your wife to send one of her apple pies with you."

"I think that can be arranged."

Another customer entered, and Kristi turned to see Martin Pritchard. Her stomach clenched. Martin had been trying to buy her family's land for as long as she could remember. He had nearly succeeded when her grandfather had fallen behind on his taxes two years earlier, an oversight that had occurred only months before his death.

"Kristi. I thought you were turning into a recluse on that island of yours." The sneer in Martin's voice reminded her of what she wanted to forget. If the lawsuit in November didn't go her way, the island would no longer be hers. It would be his.

Forcing some confidence into her words, she said, "If I could get Bill to deliver my mail, I might do just that." She slid her credit card into the card reader to pay for her postage.

"Winter's coming. You sure you can handle being out there all by yourself?" Martin asked.

"I'll manage." She collected her receipt and turned toward the wall of post office boxes. "Thanks, Bill."

Fighting against the uncertainty of the future, she unlocked her box, collected her mail, and walked outside. While she normally spent time walking through town and visiting various shops, the storm clouds in the distance and Martin's presence in town were enough to dissuade her. Instead, she started down the street toward the market, glancing around as she walked.

Carol Alston wiped down the outdoor tables of the café. Outside the barber shop, Bruce Wiedelmyer chatted with Lowell Hansen, the owner of the butcher shop. Apparently, Lowell was serious about forcing his son, Grant, to take over the business. This was the third time in two weeks she had seen Lowell outside his shop.

Mayor Gilsom strolled out of the café, accompanied by the town manager, Vincent Anders. Kristi hoped she wasn't about to get cornered into another conversation about why she wasn't still dating the mayor's son. Three weeks together had been more than enough to convince her that the younger Gilsom was best suited for someone who wanted to spend her days primping in front of the mirror and her nights at whatever social event could be found.

Both men stopped to greet her.

"Kristi, it's been too long since you've been out to the house. We're going to have to remedy that," Stuart Gilsom said, shaking her hand.

Kristi nearly smiled at the mayor's predictability. "I gather Monte is back in town."

"Didn't you hear? He'll be starting his residency at the regional hospital next week." Pride dripped from the mayor's voice.

"That's great. You must be thrilled to have him so close."

"I am. I thought you might be pleased with the news as well," Stuart said. "You two do make a handsome couple."

"We *did* make a handsome couple," Kristi corrected. "You just want him to settle down with someone around here so you can keep him close to home."

"Can you blame me?" Stuart asked.

"Not at all." The wind kicked up, and Kristi tugged on her ball cap to keep it in place. "Is everything else going well?"

"Can't complain. Vincent here is trying to keep me on track."

"No easy task," Kristi said.

"No, it isn't," Vincent agreed. "Sometimes I think it was easier when the mayor here was fixing the town instead of running it."

"Once an engineer, always an engineer," Stuart said good-naturedly.

"So you keep telling me," Vincent said.

Ignoring his town manager's comment, the mayor focused on Kristi again. "Kristi, why don't you come over for dinner tonight? My wife said something about grilling some steaks."

"Thanks, but I want to get home before this storm rolls in," Kristi said.

"And we'd better get back to the office." Vincent motioned to town hall. "See you later, Kristi."

The two men crossed the street and stopped to chat with Bruce and Lowell before continuing toward the town hall. Heading down the sidewalk, Kristi made her way into the market and retrieved a cart. Even though she had shopped earlier this week, it wouldn't be long before the weather would keep her from coming to town often.

She loaded up on various canned and dried food, as well as numerous baking items and a few perishables. When she reached the single checkout counter, she greeted the cashier. "Hey, Stacy. How's it going?"

The pretty redhead flipped her long hair over her shoulders. "Brad Mayweather asked me out yesterday."

"That's great." Kristi unloaded her purchases onto the counter and let herself fall into the lazy cadence of small-town conversation. "You've had your eye on him for a while now."

"Ever since Lily broke up with him. Did you hear she's engaged to that banker she's been dating?"

"The one in Augusta?"

"Yeah. Rumor has it that he's put in for a transfer to the branch here. Lily doesn't want to move away, especially after that cancer scare with her dad last year."

"I don't blame her," Kristi said, fighting the regret that always swept over her whenever she thought of her grandfather and the missed opportunities she'd had for visits when he was still alive.

Stacy rang up a case of canned milk. "Maybe you should invest in a cow."

"I've thought about it," Kristi admitted. "But then I would have to milk it every day. Not sure I'm ready to go to that extreme to be self-sufficient."

"Speaking of which, do you have any more of that blueberry pie filling you made?" Stacy asked. "We had some requests for it yesterday."

"I have about a dozen more cases I can sell."

"Can you bring them next time you come into town? Might as well get them in stock before the weather turns."

"No problem." Kristi paid for her purchases. "Is it okay if I borrow the cart to take this stuff to my boat?"

"Of course."

"Thanks. I'll see you later." Kristi pushed her cart outside and walked the two blocks to the harbor. Her eyes swept over the boats docked there, her gaze landing on the only unfamiliar vessel, a white cabin cruiser. A man stood at the helm, a hat hiding his face. He turned away from her as though staring out at the harbor.

His gray, long-sleeved T-shirt rippled in the wind, his toned back and shoulders evident. He turned his head slightly, and her breath caught, a memory from the past flooding through her.

She had been so young when Ace Samson had become the center of her world. His death had stolen what was left of her carefree days, leaving behind a scar that had never completely healed.

Her chest tight, she shook her head, fighting against the heartache and the sense of loss that could still sneak up on her unexpectedly.

She loaded her groceries into her boat and returned the cart to the store. When she returned, she glanced at the man on the cabin cruiser, again reminded of the happy memories of the man who had first captured her heart.

Eager to get on the water, she cast off. The sky darkened, her mood darkening with it. Life with Ace had been so bright, so promising, but every time she thought of him, she couldn't help but remember the moment her future had died with him.

* * *

Ace followed the boat with the bright-blue sails, his body tensing each time Kristi came into view. She hadn't lost her touch on the water, constantly finessing the edge of the wind to give herself more speed over the waves.

Taking a parallel path, he followed her general direction while trying to maintain the appearance that he was heading back down the coast. Storm clouds threatened in the distance. He hoped he didn't have to travel far.

To his relief, Kristi adjusted her course and headed for land. An island. He hadn't expected that.

She maneuvered toward a small inlet on the wayward side of the crescent-shaped piece of land located a mile off the coast of Maine. Ace glanced behind him, taking note of the two other vessels in the vicinity. One appeared to be heading toward the village, and the other was a fishing boat at anchor.

Continuing his course, Ace waited until he was out of sight of Kristi's sailboat before he circled the island.

He scanned for any signs of life, not seeing anything besides a single doe on the edge of the woods. Taking his time, he rounded the curve of land to where he had started and studied the quiet cove with a single dock protruding into its center.

Kristi's boat bobbed in the water, the sails secure. A picturesque cottage sat nestled in the trees a short distance from the natural beach, a larger home spanning the bluff to the right.

The wraparound porch and stairs leading to the beach and dock evoked an air of hospitality, yet from a defensive standpoint, he found himself approving. No one could approach this side of the island without the occupants seeing the newcomers, and the trees had been thinned out on the other side of the house so natural predators would be easily noticed as well.

A door opened, and a black lab bounded down the stairs of the main house. Ace slowed his speed and angled toward the dock.

"Samson!" Kristi called out.

Ace froze for a brief moment before he realized she was talking to the dog. The dog didn't slow, apparently eager to greet the island's newest guest.

Ace cut the engine and tied off his boat.

"Samson!" she called again. Kristi appeared at the railing and froze the moment she saw Ace. "Can I help you?"

Ace finished securing his boat and stepped onto the dock. "I hope so."

He started toward the stairs, leaving his hat in place as a last-ditch effort to remain anonymous until he knew how many people were living on this island. The dog trotted along beside him, nosing his hand as though trying to get Ace to pet him. The feel of soft fur beneath his fingers chased away the worst of his nerves. "He's not much of a guard dog, is he?"

"Who are you?" Kristi asked. A touch of uneasiness rippled through her voice when she added, "What do you want?"

Ace opened his mouth to answer her first question but couldn't quite manage it. "I have a job offer I want to discuss," he said instead. He reached the bottom of the stairs and ran a hand over the dog's head. Drawing up his courage, he removed his hat and lifted his eyes to meet hers. "It's good to see you again, Kristi."

"Do I know you?"

Ace remained silent, giving her time to study the forty-year-old version of the man she had once loved. He saw the moment recognition dawned. Surprise, disbelief, confusion, hurt. So many emotions flickered across her face, but only one word escaped her lips. "Ace."

CHAPTER 3

KRISTI SHOOK HER HEAD IN disbelief. Could this man really be Ace Samson, the man she had spent the past two decades mourning? How was it possible? She had been at the funeral. She had watched his coffin be lowered into the ground in the cemetery outside Bangor, the same place she went twice a year to place flowers on his grave.

Seconds passed, stretching into minutes. Her mind raced, all the while the man who appeared to be her long-lost love stood patiently in her yard, hat in hand.

Finally, she managed to form words. "I don't understand."

He shifted his weight from one foot to the other. "May I come in?"

Certain she must be mistaken, she stepped forward. Her knees wobbled on the first step, her hand gripping the railing as she steadied herself. She descended slowly, her gaze remaining on him. Three steps from the bottom, she saw the dark circle around his irises and the spot of brown in his left eye that interrupted the green. Her own eyes flooded as reality came into focus. "Ace!"

Pure joy replaced her disbelief, and she rushed forward, her arms outstretched. Surprise registered on his face, replaced quickly by relief an instant before he welcomed her into his embrace.

Kristi's fingers curled into his cotton sweatshirt, and she breathed in his scent. It wasn't the familiar mix of Old Spice and ocean, but the arms holding her close brought back the rush of memories of life before Ace had died.

She let herself revel in his presence, in the strength of his arms around her. Her memories brought more tears to her eyes, their time apart creeping into her thoughts. Swallowing hard, she pulled back and looked up at the chiseled jawline and the two-day beard that shadowed his face. "It's really you. I thought . . ." Her voice trailed off, and she tried again. "The police said . . ."

"I know. I'm sorry."

Kristi reached up and pressed her hands to his cheeks, her eyes meeting his. The remorse she read there pierced her elation at finding him alive, questions surfacing along with the memories of the two decades she had suffered without him. Hurt and betrayal slowly overshadowed her other tangled emotions. "Where have you been?" she finally managed to ask. "Why did you let me think you were dead all this time?"

"I'm sorry," he said again.

The simple apology spurred a new flood of emotions, but none of them resembled forgiveness. She took a step back.

Her breath backed up in her lungs, every muscle tightening. Again, her words wouldn't come. For two decades, he had been living a lie that had altered everything for both of them. New tears trickled onto her cheeks, and she repeated her question. "All these years. How could you let me think you were dead?"

"I couldn't tell you the truth."

"What truth?" she managed to ask. "Every birthday, every anniversary of your death, I've been at your graveside, wishing for what could have been. I mourned you all this time, and now I find out I was the worst kind of fool."

"You've never been a fool."

As though sensing her need for every ounce of support available, Samson left Ace and brushed against her leg.

A boat sounded in the distance, and Ace edged closer. "Please, can we go inside?"

Though part of her wanted to send him away out of spite, logic chased that instinct away. She wanted answers. She needed answers.

Her emotions were in turmoil, but she waved toward the house and started up the stairs. The sound of footsteps behind her reinforced the fact that Ace Samson wasn't a ghost.